I0722197

DEVIL Deal

Janina Franck

Crimson Fox
PUBLISHING

DEVIL DEAL

First Edition

Copyright @ 2022 by Janina Franck
www.janinafranck.com

Published by Crimson Fox Publishing,
PO Box 1035, Turner, OR 97392, USA
www.CrimsonFoxPublishing.com

Cover art: Rebecacovers

All rights reserved. This book or any portion thereof
may not be reproduced or used in any manner
whatsoever without the express written permission
of the author except for the use of brief quotations in
a book review.

This is a work of fiction. Names, characters, places,
and incidents are the products of the author's
imagination. Any resemblance to actual persons,
living or dead, businesses, companies, events, or
locales is entirely coincidental.

ISBN (e-book): 978-1-952667-90-9
ISBN (paperback): 978-1-952667-91-6

For Trina and Sam.

May your love be eternal.

Chapter 1

The absolute stupidest thing any living person in this world can do is to make a deal with the Devil.

Here's the thing — I'm the *queen* of bad decisions.

I'm sure you can do basic arithmetic. That's right. One plus one equals I jumped at the chance when the opportunity presented itself. And having a deal with the Devil comes with no end of trouble, believe you me.

"Don't you have anything to make cocktails?"

"Not since you raided my shelves last," I said sullenly, leaning against my marble-top kitchen isle, cup of tea in hands while watching Luce shift through my cupboards determinedly, his white shirt rolled up to his sleeves, revealing the winding tattoo of intertwining vines on his muscular left forearm. "But if you want tea, I've got you covered." I nodded toward the corner of my kitchen counter that was reserved for my roughly estimated fifty thousand types of loose-leaf tea boxes.

Luce barely turned around to scrunch his nose at me. "Don't you at least have coffee?"

I squinted at the ceiling, trying to remember if I

had bought coffee for any of my guests within the last few years. I hated the stuff myself. Wouldn't be caught dead with it. But there had been that one guy last year—full beard, flannel shirts… The kind of guy who only drank draft beers and special-blend coffee and went to the farmer's market every weekend. Pretty sure he'd been talking about going vegan, too. I thought I might have bought some coffee for him.

"There might be some instant in the drawer over there." I pointed, and Luce rushed over, almost breaking the darn thing as he yanked it open. He pulled out an untouched packet of instant coffee, still neatly wrapped in plastic. The guy never had touched it, had he? I supposed it hadn't been fancy enough for him. Well, I'd tried. Sorta.

"Oh, thank the smoldering depths!" Luce sighed in relief. Mildly amused, I watched him prepare the disgusting brew he so craved. Normally, Luce brought his coffee with him when he arrived, so somehow this had never come up as an issue before.

My attention was quickly diverted by my buzzing phone.

Reminder: 2morro @ 14:00 sharp! Don't you dare b l8!
L

I'd already marked the appointment in big, fat red letters in my calendar. There was not a chance in Hell I was going to miss Lynn trying on bridal gowns. She'd look far too cute, and not to mention beautiful, for me to miss it. Besides, there was going to be free champagne. Have you ever heard a girl pass up free champagne?

Yeah. I didn't think so.

Besides, it was my duty as her best friend and maid of honor, and after all she had done for me over the years, I was going to be the best bridesmaid she could ever dream of having.

K.

After hitting "send," I slipped my phone back in my pocket to find Luce staring at me, cradling his coffee.

"Are you enjoying life?" he asked.

I looked back at him with a blank expression. "What?"

"Are you making the most of it?" he elaborated. "I don't want you to die having regrets and all, since you're gonna go... y'know..." He jerked his thumb down.

I only raised an eyebrow.

After he continued to watch me intensely, I sighed and tucked a strand of my black hair behind my ear. "I'm good, okay? Stop worrying so much." I smirked at him. "You're gonna make me think you actually care."

He smirked right back at me. "Well, I guess we can't have that now, can we?" He finally took a sip of his coffee and shrugged. "Fine."

I glanced at my watch. Time to head to work.

"Do me a favor and leave the window cracked

open when you go home." I walked around the kitchen island to grab my cheap, yet surprisingly durable, knock-off bag and keys. "I don't want the smell lingering."

Luce saluted smartly in response.

"Oh, Ames!" he called out as I headed out the door. I poked my head back in the kitchen. "Let me know when you're ready for me to set you up."

He grinned that blindingly devilish grin of his, the one that suited his milk-coffee-colored complexion so well, the kind that made most people swoon at the sight of it.

I rolled my eyes. "When Hell freezes over."

"I can arrange for that, you know."

"But I don't think your daddy would let you."

He scowled at me. "That's foul play," he grumbled. "Leave my dad out of it."

Instead of letting myself be pulled into a long, drawn-out discussion on the matter, I just headed out, only yelling "Byeeee" into the hallway before the front door shut and locked behind me.

I wished I had skipped work. Instead of getting cracking on my backlog of analyses, my boss, Carol, had handed me a new person to train within five minutes of arriving. Why that task suddenly fell to me, I had no idea. Maybe Carol was busy. Maybe she was hoping my past experiences as secretary slash office manager in a smaller company would help me give this new hire a few good insider tips. Kit, as she told me she liked to be called, was fresh out of college and had not been hired for her brains, as I realized quickly through our interactions. Still, she seemed like a nice young woman. And if everyone handled her with kid gloves, she'd be doing just fine as office manager. In this place, it shouldn't be too tough anyway.

Kit had a slender figure and was about my height, though her childlike behavior made her seem shorter. Her outfit, made up of impractical heels and a bright red dress that matched her lipstick, drew a lot of attention as I showed her around the office, introducing her to people. Many gazes lingered on her for longer than was strictly polite. After ensuring she'd met everyone she needed to know from day one in order to do her job, I took her to the kitchen.

"You can get coffee here, or tea if you prefer," I told her, "and over there you can grab fresh fruit whenever. Any questions so far?"

"Um, yeah." She giggled, batting her brown eyes as she twirled a long, strawberry-blonde curl around one finger. "Do you, like, have a pool here?"

I stared at her in disbelief. "Huh?"

"A pool, or a massage chair. You know, my friend, she works at Google, and she told me that they have a pool *and* a massage chair *and* free breakfast, and they even get video games on loan for free."

She smiled innocently at me, but I could only stare back at her blankly.

"A pool," I repeated, trying to wrap my head around the fact that she was comparing our company to Google. She nodded earnestly. "No," I said slowly. "We do not have a pool. We don't have a massage chair, either."

"Oh." Her lips dropped into a pout.

"But you get free drinks and fresh fruit every day—that's pretty cool?" I gestured at the kitchen.

Kit pursed her lips and looked across the room. "I guess," she said, visibly crestfallen.

I shook my head, trying to wrap my head around her expectations. She hadn't even been here for a whole day yet!

"Okay, let's get you some training. Amanda should be done setting up your computer now." I didn't wait to see if she'd follow me. I just marched out and straight through the office to her desk, sadly close to mine. I could see from here that my phone was blinking to inform me of missed calls, and I would have bet a fortune on emails having piled up by the dozens every minute I'd spent with Kit. I didn't mind training her, but I wished I'd have gotten some kind of advanced notice so I could have prepared for it. Right now, it was just unnecessarily causing me more stress.

"Um, what's the security code?" Her words

ripped me from sullen thoughts, only to throw me a curve ball. Her screen was displaying the message that should only pop up when the wrong password had been inserted three times.

"Kit," I asked, trying to remain calm and patient. "Do you know what your password is meant to be yet?"

"No," she said cheerfully. "That's why it didn't work, I guess. What's the security code?"

I had to restrain myself from wiping my hand across my face. "Why would you try to enter a password if you don't know what it is?"

She shrugged. "I thought it might mean the one I use for my computer at home. Or a trick question and there is no password. But neither of them worked, so I tried to make up a new one."

Her smile was radiant. But I was starting to wonder if there was a brain hidden behind that almost snow-white forehead of hers.

This was going to be a long, long day.

I drove back home to my house at the end of a lovely cul-de-sac, exhausted from training Kit and having to explain the simplest things without losing my patience. That last part had truly been the most difficult of them all. Never mind that I'd also had to stay late to get the most vital parts of my actual work done before the weekend. Not how I'd hoped the day would go.

Frustrated, I slammed my bag on the kitchen counter before I put away the mess Luce had left behind, starting with his used cup.

"Honey, I'm home," I said quietly to myself. Sarcastically, obviously.

The house was empty. *Maybe I should get a cat.* Dogs felt like too much work. They were nice to pet and all, but all the attention I'd have to give them? Ugh, don't sign me up for that. Then again, I'd probably be a terrible pet owner even for a cat. I'd just forget to clean the litter box, or quite possibly even to feed it.

I grimaced at the thought. No pets for me.

Besides, I had Luce. And he was so much more work than a pet could ever be. With all his shenanigans and random pop-ups, I had my hands full.

I recalled a hairy situation last year, right around the time that thing with the coffee guy had gone haywire, where we'd worried that he might have gotten some woman pregnant. It wasn't very likely thanks to his heritage, but it was certainly possible. Any cat I might have had around that time would have left and never looked back—or have starved to death. Luce had *not* been pleased about his dubious genes potentially being passed on.

I opened the fridge—nothing worthy of notice.

Closing it, I pulled out a random restaurant flyer from the stack under a fridge magnet. A moment later, I was dialing the number for a Japanese restaurant's delivery service. The moment the first ring came through, I could sense Luce's presence—along with an unpleasant waft of rotten eggs that luckily faded quickly thanks to the open window.

"Sashiminiki," an unenthusiastic voice droned out of the speaker. "May I take your order?"

Luce practically jumped into my field of vision, signing me that he wanted in. I nodded as I gave the restaurant our usual order.

When I hung up, I turned around to find Luce plonking a tiny crystal figurine on the counter. No, not crystal. Ice. It was already forming a puddle.

"Eh?" He gestured at it enthusiastically.

"What are you trying to do?" I asked, equal amounts puzzled and amused.

"It's ice," he said, by way of explanation.

"I can see that." I stepped closer to take a better look. It was a figurine of himself, unsurprisingly, holding a mace in what I assumed he'd meant to be a seductive manner. "What I mean is, why?"

"I made Hell freeze over."

I glanced up at him. "Um… I hate to sound like a broken record, but… why?"

He dropped his arms and crossed them in front of his chest, pouting. "So you'll agree to let me set you up, obviously. It's about time you get back on that horse."

"No, thanks," I said quickly. "There's no way I'm letting you set me up."

"Why not?" He looked so disappointed. Like a puppy that had had its favorite chew toy taken away. "I couldn't possibly find someone worse for you than you did yourself."

Oof. He really knew where to prick so it hurt. But he wasn't wrong. After all, my choice in men was the reason I was here, chatting with the Devil in my very kitchen. And from the few years I'd known him, I knew he wasn't going to give up on this easily.

I sighed, pushing him out of the way so I could saunter to the living room and drop on the couch. "I'll think about it."

I didn't end up thinking about it. Mostly because we spent the rest of the evening watching bad movies. Like, really bad movies. The kind that were so bad that they were good again—provided you watched them with the right people. And, well, Luce had proven to be "the right people" on many occasions.

I didn't know what compelled him to come see me as often as he did when our deal had backfired on me. After all, I knew for a fact that it wasn't normal Devil behavior and definitely nothing that had any impact on our deal. But he'd stuck around. Helped me pick up the pieces of my shattered heart and shown me the way to move on. And somewhere along the way I'd started to think of him as my friend.

Don't judge me—hanging out with him was fun, okay? Devil or not.

"Want some ice cream?" I asked when we had finished the first movie—and our dinner.

He reflected on my offer theatrically. "Ice cream…" His spread fingertips came together softly and parted again as he frowned at the ceiling. I watched him patiently. It shouldn't take long for him to say that he wanted some.

When I'd first met him, it had been in his Devil shape. He had three shapes: his Devil form, his human form, and his angel form. You'd be surprised to learn which one of them was the scariest. Hint: It wasn't the Devil form.

As a human, he looked normal—incredibly handsome, sure, with his luscious, dark hair and equally dark eyes, but nevertheless like an ordinary person. And one with good fashion sense, too. Usually, he liked wearing either white or blue shirts neatly tucked into his jeans. A respectable outfit for most occasions. Even now, lounging on my couch, he didn't bother changing into something more comfortable like I had. Next to him, I looked like a bog gremlin in my sweats and messy bun.

"Ice cream?" he repeated quietly to himself, narrowing his eyes as if it were a tough decision. "Ice cream," he eventually confirmed with a slow nod. "With a dash of Bailey's."

He was damned lucky I had hidden some of the stuff in my basement fridge.

On my way down the stairs, my phone buzzed in my pocket. I glanced at it, but upon seeing an unknown number, I decided not to answer. Anyone whom I didn't have saved on my phone shouldn't be calling me on it. They shouldn't even have the number. If they needed to get in touch with me for any reason, they could just call the landline my uncle had installed way back when. Or send an email like a normal person. Heck, I'd probably even accept a text or conventional letter. But no random caller was going to wreck my Friday night, as uneventful as it might be.

Just as I was going through the freezer to look for the ice cream, I heard a sudden thudding sound from upstairs. Grabbing both the ice cream and Bailey's quickly, I rushed back up.

"Luce? What did you knock over this time? Please tell me it's not the TV!" My shout received no reply. In fact, I didn't hear much of anything. "Luce?"

I entered the living room—empty. No one was here. The lamp next to the couch where Luce had been just minutes earlier had been knocked to the floor, though.

Before I had time to really contemplate what had just happened, and why Luce had gone, the doorbell rang. I really couldn't catch a break tonight, could I? What was with these constant interruptions?

With a sigh, I deposited my loot from the basement on the table and made to open the front door, only sparing a brief moment to glance somewhat annoyed at my subpar appearance in the hallway mirror.

"Can I help you?" I said to the two men wearing black suits and sunglasses, even though it was night. So douchey. "Let me guess, you're gonna tell me you're from the FBI or something?"

I'd meant it to be a joke, but neither one of them smiled.

"Miss Amelia Perez?" The one who spoke looked like he was in his late forties, maybe even fifties. There were streaks of grey in his hair, but not enough to be very noticeable. He was so white, he may as well have been a ghost.

"That's me." Impatiently, I tapped the doorframe. "What'cha got for me?"

The other one, white with a dash of tanning studio, craned his head trying to look into the house past me. Raising an eyebrow, I stepped into his line of sight while pulling the door a little into their way.

The first guy cleared his throat.

"We're here to check for gas leaks," he said. "We realize the timing might be inconvenient, but it's for your own safety, you understand."

A gas leak?

"Oh yeah?" Skeptical, I searched both their faces for information. "Who sent you?"

"Excuse me?" He seemed genuinely startled by my question, so I graciously repeated it for him.

"Which organization do you work for?"

"Oh, uh, Gas Networks, of course."

I narrowed my eyes. "So you rang my doorbell while suspecting a gas leak in my home?"

The two glanced at each other. Tanning-Studio shrugged. "Well, yes."

No way. One of the first pieces of advice found online about gas leaks was not to use any form of electrical appliances, *including doorbells*, if one suspected a gas leak. I knew, because I'd looked it up because I kept smelling rotten eggs back when Luce first came into my life and I'd been concerned about it. No way a professional would have risked it. Which meant that I didn't trust these two farther than I could throw them. Which… wasn't very far. Or at all. I'd never really been all that much into fitness, though I told myself every few months that I'd start going to the gym.

"Well, I'm sure it's okay," I chirped. "I've not noticed anything strange. Have a good day!"

I moved to close the door in their faces, but White-as-a-Ghost-Face slipped his foot between door and frame. I could hear the tiniest yelp when the door hit his foot.

"Excuse me, there must be some misunderstanding. But you see, we have to do our job—we can't go back to our boss without something to show for it. You understand, right? Won't you just let us take a reading? It's always best to be safe."

His voice was pleading but spending a lot of time with the Devil had taught me to smell a scam from three miles away.

I opened the door again, beaming at the two of them. "Well, when you put it that way… You're right, of course. Please come on in!"

I waited just long enough for White-Face to pull his foot back in relief.

"When I've moved out," I added darkly, and I slammed the door, immediately engaging knob lock and the deadbolt.

I stalked back to the living room and grabbed my inhaler to take a hit before starting another movie on the TV, turning the volume so high I couldn't hear the doorbell or the shouts outside anymore. I didn't know what kind of scam they wanted to pull, and, frankly, I didn't care. I wasn't overly concerned about Luce disappearing, either. He did that sometimes. He might also pop up again any time from two seconds to two months from now. Right now, I was only concerned with whether the clown on screen was going to murder that child… Oh, yup. The kid was dead.

Chapter 2

After smashing my alarm back into silence about half a dozen times, I finally rolled out of bed. Literally. And I pulled the blanket with me. The floor was hard and cold, which made waking up a little easier than the warm comfort of my bed, and I finally sat up, blearily staring at the room at large while I waited for my eyes to get accustomed to the light and my brain to return from dreamland.

I yawned heartily. Okay. Time to get ready. It might only be ten o'clock, and I needed to meet Lynn at two, but I needed to look my best for the fitting, needed to make sure to get a good breakfast in so I could handle the champagne, and then there was still the one-hour drive to the store to consider. Never even mind traffic or the fact that I was going to have to be early to escape Lynn's bridal wrath. Ugh, I should probably take a taxi instead of taking my own car. Inconvenient though it was, I refused to drive if I was drinking.

Getting myself ready and fed turned out to be faster and easier than I expected. Apparently, I was less maintenance than I'd thought. The drive, however, was threatening to suck the soul right out of my body. Glaring at the drivers honking their horns all around us, I contemplated whether I should have taken the bus after all, despite it being a pain. Then again, it probably wouldn't have made me arrive much faster.

The traffic jam crept forward so slowly, I figured I might walk and get there faster. Hell, I could probably walk home and back before I'd get there by car!

Checking the time when we came to a complete stop, I realized that it was already one-thirty, and I was only a quarter of the way there. Yeah, there was no chance I'd make it on time.

"Hey," I said to the driver, "do you think we could take a different route to get out of this? And maybe get there before two P.M.?"

He glanced at me through the review mirror, his gaze stony and about as annoyed as I felt. "I'll try."

All his tone said was that I'd just slashed the rating he was going to give me down to one star.

"Thanks," I said.

Somehow the driver managed to get to the bridal store only fifteen minutes late. As expected, Lynn was fuming, her curly black hair tied back into a ponytail as she glared at me with her almost golden-brown eyes. "I *told* you not to be late, Amy!"

I lifted my hands in defense. "Hey, I didn't know there was going to be this busy today! Plus, there was an accident on the way!"

"They call it a being prepared? Besides, with all the traffic apps out there, you'd think you could have checked one, at least!"

I gave up on defending myself to her. She wasn't entirely wrong, and as a bride-to-be, I supposed I had to give her some leniency on her mood. She'd met me just outside the store, and I followed her in, where her mother, Grace—wearing her usual business suit with a shirt that belonged into the eighteen hundreds—her work friend Brianna—a tall, brunette in a simple blouse and jeans—and her future sister-in-law, Hailey—a young blonde woman wearing pink dungarees in combination with sparkly heels—were already waiting, seated on a luxurious cream-colored couch, each with a glass of champagne in hand. I gave them all a brief nod.

Lynn's thunderous mood dissipating as quickly as a summer storm, she beamed at the store's owner, a mousey white woman with insanely good posture hovering nearby. "Let's start."

I shot her a surprised glance. She'd actually waited for me to get here before starting? *Aww!*

As her mother, almost sister-in-law, and Brianna got up and walked over to inspect some of the dresses on hangers, Lynn turned back to me.

"My idea for today was this: Each one of you picks out a dress you think would look good on me, and I'll try them all on. Whoever finds the dress I choose, will be my maid or matron of honor." She grinned at me winningly before leaning in and lowering her voice conspiratorially. "Please, please pick something good. Don't let either one of those two win."

I nodded, though I had to admit I was puzzled. So far, I'd been under the assumption that I was her maid of honor already, being her best friend and all. But I supposed she had to make some concessions to other people. I wasn't exactly her family's favorite person—something I had Luce and an extremely embarrassing dinner party to thank for. Though my own rather direct personality might also have been part of the reason.

I was also surprised that Lynn had included Grace in the competition since it wasn't all that usual to have one's mother be a matron of honor. Then again, I was no expert on the subject and Lynn had never been one to do things the "usual" way.

Still, I was intent on doing the best I could for her, so I turned my attention to the tulle and silks. After looking at what felt like hundreds of dresses, of which many were completely unsuitable for Lynn's darker skin tone, I finally found it. It was perfect.

Without looking around further or overthinking it, I handed it to the owner of the store to put into the changing room for Lynn and took a seat on the couch while I waited for everyone else to finish up as well.

I soon realized that I should have brought a book.

It seemed like the other women were intent on inspecting every single dress in the store, including Lynn. At least she was only doing it to pass the time. Turned out they could easily have started on the "contest" before I'd gotten here.

I pulled out my phone to find a missed call from an unknown number. They hadn't left a message. Deciding that I had more than enough time to waste on irrelevant things, I clicked on callback.

Beep. Beep. Beep. Beep.

Doo, doo, doo.

"This number is not in service."

I glared at my phone as if it had insulted my entire family line with its friendly female voice. *Ugh.* I should have known better than to actually try to call back what was presumably a telemarketing scam out of boredom. Before I had the chance to throw my phone on the ground or do anything equally stupid, Lynn plopped onto the couch next to me. "You must be pretty confident if you're already sitting around," she said, peering into my face curiously.

I smirked at her. "You bet I am. It's gonna take a lot to beat the dress I chose."

"Hm." She leaned back, and her lips curled up in amusement. "If you say so. But if it sucks, you better believe that you'll be wearing a wedding dress that's just as bad when it's your turn."

"My turn?" I raised an eyebrow at her and snorted. "Unlikely."

Suddenly, her smile dropped, and her brows furrowed as her gaze turned into pure compassion, and she took my hand, squeezing it tightly.

"Amy, I know it's been… tough since Jonathan, but… you need to move on. You deserve a happily ever after, too, you know."

She gave me a sad smile, accompanied by an endearing puppy-dog look. Nevertheless, I stiffened at the name she'd mentioned.

Jonathan. The man who'd been *meant* to be my happily-ever-after. But now, thanks to that very same guy, that was something unattainable for me.

"Why don't you let me set you up?" Lynn apparently read the hurt in my eyes, the wound that reopened every once in a while, because she squeezed my hand again and returned to her usual chirpy self. "You know I won't let you sit on your own at my wedding. You're going to have a date, and it can be either someone of your choosing, or someone I pick out for you."

"I'll think about it," I grumbled, awkwardly reminded of my conversation with Luce just the previous night. "But how about we go back to focusing on you now?"

At that, she perked up and looking around the store. "Everyone ready?"

Brianna raced through the shop from the other end and pushed a dress into the clerk's hands.

"Yes," she gasped, as the others nodded.

Lynn winked at me and followed the clerk to the changing room. The other women took their seats next to me on the couch and all of us picked up our champagne glasses, sipping away at our drinks politely as though this weren't really a competition we all wanted to win. I felt the looks the other three were throwing me and each other, almost as though they were sizing each other up, but I ignored them, waiting patiently for Lynn to come out again. After all, I was confident I knew what she would love.

"Ready?" the clerk asked as she popped out of the changing room. We all nodded.

A moment later, Lynn glided out, eliciting gasps from the other women, her dress a brilliant white mermaid-shape with lace shaped like flower petals adorning the bust and waist, seeping into the skirt around Lynn's hips. Inset into the lace were sparkling stones and glitter, to really draw attention to the low décolleté. Ordinarily this would have been a beautiful dress, but it was made for a white woman, as evidenced by the rose-colored skin-tone sleeves full of glitter.

I had no doubts that it had been picked by her fiancée's sister, Hailey, a girl so white, she was practically the poster image. She had a *trust fund.* However, even though the dress was beautiful, and the sleeves could probably be changed to match Lynn's dark skin tone, it wasn't the right dress for her. Not because it didn't look good, but because it didn't match her personality. Lynn was like me—she wanted to be able to *move*—something that was difficult to do in a mermaid dress. Plus, also like me, she wasn't much of a glitter-and-sparkles person.

After inspecting herself from all sides, Lynn nodded without a word and presented herself to us again. "Your opinions, ladies?"

Hailey was the first to announce her approval. "It's stunning—it looks amazing on you. Like, you could totally be a princess."

Lynn only granted her a mild smile. I was impressed by her laid-back attitude. As far as I knew, most women would get teary when seeing themselves in a wedding dress for the first time, even if it wasn't the perfect one. But she was the same as always. Laid-back and easygoing.

"I'm not completely sure about the sleeves," Brianna said, grimacing slightly. "But otherwise, it looks lovely on you."

Lynn's gaze moved to her mom, who only shook her head. Then she set on me.

"No way." I could have outlined why I didn't like it, but I didn't need to. After all, Lynn was the one who'd make the decision either way. She just wanted to know what we thought.

She turned back toward the dressing room. "Next dress!"

This time, the other women put a pause on sizing up one another, though Hailey still glared the occasional dagger at me with crossed arms and pouty lips. Perhaps even more so than before. Brianna began pacing again, looking at more dresses hanging in the store, while Grace started flipping through a bridal magazine laid out on the table. I pulled out my phone again and wrote a text to Luce.

Gonna need drinks 2nite. Beetlejuice?

His reply came promptly. Exactly how he managed to get service in Hell was a mystery to me, but hey, I wasn't complaining. It sure made it easier to get in touch with him. Well. When he wanted to reply, anyhow.

Pick you up at 8.

I grinned at his response. He could go out any night he wanted, and I knew he did sometimes, but more often than not, he seemed to not want to go without me. I knew because most nights he hung out with me at home. I had to admit it felt nice to get some loyalty from the Devil.

I contemplated asking Lynn to join us, but I had a feeling she might be exhausted after all the getting changed in and out of wedding dresses and prefer to spend some quiet time with her fiancée, Taylor. From what she'd told me, Taylor, like Lynn, had been busy a lot with work recently, trying to work overtime so they would not only have the money for their wedding, but also for their honeymoon. It would also allow her to take the time off for the trip they were planning. Besides, they would need the money soon.

They weren't going to waste a lot of time before trying to conceive and babies were expensive.

As if she'd heard my thoughts, she came out again in another snow-white dress designed to present her as a maiden pure of heart and body. I didn't know who had chosen it, but it was hideous. A princess cut with puff sleeves—who wore puffed sleeves in this century?—and intricate stitching all around the skirt, shaped mostly like rhombuses and triangles. It was an atrocity of modern art meets medieval princess. The outfit was completed by long, white satin gloves and an angular, asymmetrical low-cut back, right above the largest decorative bow I had ever seen.

My voice and words had been taken from me, stolen away by the sight of a wedding abomination. I could only stare. And oh, boy, did I stare. My mouth almost hit the floor, I stared so hard. Who even designed a dress like that? I glanced to the store owner, but her eyes were fixed on Lynn, a smugly satisfied expression painted on her face.

Lynn did a twirl before raising an eyebrow at us. "Well?" she asked.

"It's so unique!" Brianna spoke first, smiling genuinely. "I like that it's different to the norm."

Lynn's mom nodded along and beamed at her daughter. "I think it accentuates your best features. It's a dress that'll make your special moment all that more special, hon."

Ah, there was the culprit. I'd always known Grace

to be a little eccentric, but I'd never expected her to force her crimes against fashion on her daughter.

"It's a pretty… weird dress," Hailey said. "And I don't know if it… like… works with your body shape?"

Lynn's eyes wandered to me, and I finally caught my breath.

"Fuck no," I asserted. "That dress deserves to be burned at the stake."

Four sets of shocked eyes landed on me, and I definitely heard gasps, but Lynn only broke into a chuckle.

"Thank you!" She sighed. "You looked so in awe, I was worried you actually liked it!"

"Are you kidding me?" I gestured wildly at the dress. "It's like the aftermath of a car crash—you want to look away, but you just… can't."

We shared a laugh, but it faded quickly when we realized that no one else was joining in. Instead, they were all still staring.

Lynn cleared her throat, sobering up quickly. "Next dress?"

As soon as she left into the changing room, the temperature in the room dropped. I had just made myself very unpopular. Brianna and Grace were whispering to each other, stealing glances my way, and Hailey was tapping her phone screen wildly, only glancing up occasionally with a sour look on her face. I decided my time and energy was best spent focusing on the champagne I hadn't yet finished. I was a little disappointed that the bottle hadn't been left on the table, so I knew the one glass was all I was going to get. Those drinks with Luce tonight were beginning to look more appealing with every passing moment.

I sighed, silently lamenting how much time I was going to have to spend with these women in the next two months. We were going to have lots of fun, I could tell. Perhaps I could convince Lynn to limit our interactions as much as possible.

Rain was starting to fall outside, pattering against the windows and ceiling. The sound was hypnotic, and it made being inside in the warmth, on a reasonably comfortable couch with a glass of champagne, all the more enjoyable. I could get used to that kind of lifestyle. Maybe I should start bringing wine with me everywhere I went—it could certainly make a lot of conversations more interesting. Or at the very least more endurable.

My gaze flitted to a window, where the water was blurring the colors together. The outside world had become not much more than a grey blob, but warm lights inside made it seem like there was no difference in here.

A few people ran through the rain outside, covering their heads pointlessly with briefcases, bags, and jackets and I felt just a little sorry for them. If I'd been at home, I'd be racing through the house closing all the windows... Crap. Was it raining over there? I'd left at least two of the windows open, hadn't I? Ugh, it was going to rain all over the floor. With any luck, Luce was helping himself to my fridge and he'd be nice enough to close them for me. I could always ask...?

I took my phone from my purse again.

Close my windows? /\((ˆ□ ˆ)*

Sent not a moment too soon. Lightning flashed, brightening up the world for an instant as a thunderous roar made the glasses on the table tremble. Wow, it had been a while since I'd heard thunder that bad. Made me wonder if one of Luce's buddies had had something to do with it. Come to think of it, I wasn't sure if demons or fallen angels could impact the weather. I should ask Luce when I next got a chance.

Before I could dwell on that thought any longer, Lynn came out wearing the next dress. This one was genuinely gorgeous.

It was a strapless tea-length dress in a light pastel-blue and a skirt that fanned out naturally. Snowflakes of lace adorned her heart-shaped décolleté, bleeding down into the top of the skirt. It was tied with elaborate knotwork along the sides, providing her with a natural corset. A belt with large crystals wrapped around her waist, completing the image of an ice princess on her wedding day. The length of the dress revealed Lynn's long, slender legs — the kind that most women would kill for.

It took me a long time to realize I was staring again, though this time because Lynn was so beautiful. The shimmering of her eyes told me that she felt the same way. Even my strong friend was overwhelmed looking so perfect. This time, she turned to me first for my opinion. With her eyes glittering with happiness and her chest expanding and contracting so visibly in her nervousness, I could do little more than smile sweetly. "It looks perfect on you."

The others were quick to nod their consent and Brianna especially beamed. She'd truly picked out a wonderful dress — it encapsulated Lynn's unique and creative personality with the grace and elegance she deserved.

Still, despite how perfect the dress looked, Lynn didn't cut the contest short, and she disappeared again to change into the last dress. The one I'd picked out for her. It had seemed perfect on the hanger, but would it look just as good on her? I'd have to wait and see.

Meanwhile, the other women were beginning to chat, the sight of Lynn as gorgeous as she was finally loosening the tension in the shop.

Their main conversation topic was the ceremony and the color schemes, along with wondering what their own dresses would be like, but I decided not to join in. The only person I really wanted to discuss those topics with was the bride—my best friend currently getting changed into the dress I had chosen for her.

It was still raining outside. Wondering if Luce had heeded my request, I pulled out my phone, only to find it dead. Crap. I'd forgotten to charge it overnight, hadn't I? Oh, well. I'd told him everything I wanted to say for the moment anyway, so it was all fine. Probably. Hm. I also couldn't summon another taxi without phone, but maybe I could get a lift home from someone here.

Lynn came out again and this time, I stopped breathing at the sight of her. If the previous dress had been perfect, this one was the dress that had invented the word. It was a cream-colored A-Line with mint-green accents. The straps were made from mint-green lace—leaved branches that stretched across her shoulders. Her back was clear, the lace only framing the sides of it as leaves, making it look like the view to the sky in a glade. On the front, a few small stones were spread across in places where the lace didn't cover, creating the illusion of stars in the night sky, the impression only enhanced by Lynn's dark skin. The laced leaves stretched into the skirt but faded out, giving way to bare cream satin.

I couldn't look away. Before long, tears were rolling across my cheeks and even through my blurry vision, I could see that Lynn fared no differently as she looked at herself in the mirror.

She turned to me with tears in her eyes. This time, I had no words to offer her. All I could do was to clasp my hands together in front of my chest and purse my lips, trying not to let the tears overwhelm me.

"Wow," Brianna breathed.

Grace shot me a look, her eyes just as full of tears as mine and Lynn's. "You picked well," she mouthed. It was the highest compliment that woman was ever going to give me, and I would take it. I nodded gratefully. Hailey was still staring.

Lynn's hands came up and flapped down again in a gesture of helplessness.

"I think we have our winner," she said, her voice trembling with emotion. She turned to me, beaming more brightly than I'd ever seen before. "Amelia Perez — will you be my maid of honor?"

I smirked back at her — surprisingly hard when your face is mushed with tears and you can barely feel your facial muscles anymore. "Was there ever any doubt?"

Chapter 3

I still felt melancholy when I unlocked my front
door and wandered into the kitchen, my ride home
courtesy of Brianna. Seeing Lynn so incredibly happy
had hit me in my soft spot. At the rate I was going—
aged thirty-one and counting—I wasn't going to
have that any time soon. Maybe ever. I knew fully
well why I'd become more cynical when it came to
love, but maybe, I thought as I made myself some
tea, just maybe… I should at least give it another
shot. Not everyone would be like Jonathan had been,
right?

I flinched when his name popped into my mind,
and I forced it out as quickly as I could. He was *not*
someone I wanted to waste any energy or effort on.
Not anymore. He'd cost me too much already.

I set my tea down to brew and climbed the stairs
to find the charger for my phone. While I was at it, I
checked the windows and noticed that they had been
closed.

Thanks, Luce, I offered in my head. He was the
best.

Having still a few hours left until he was coming

to pick me up, I decided to treat myself with a bubble bath. I deserved this after the week I'd had.

In the middle of my blissful soak, my phone, which had been playing quiet, relaxing music up until that point, buzzed and jerked me out of my peaceful trance. I glanced at the caller ID. An unknown number again. I couldn't be certain without checking, but I could have sworn that it looked an awful lot like the number I'd tried calling back a few hours ago. My curiosity mildly piqued, I picked up.

"Yup?"

"Oh, er, excuse me, am I speaking with Amelia Perez?" It was the voice of a man, though it was difficult to place his age. It was pleasant, though, friendly. But those were usually the worst strangers to call. They always wanted something.

"Who's asking?" I pulled up my knees to my chest, my mood sinking again. Maybe I shouldn't have picked up after all.

"My name is Father Exodus."

"Exodus? Like the chapter in the Bible?" I blurted out.

The voice on the other end paused for a moment before relenting, clearing his throat. "Yes, like that. So, are you Mrs. Perez?"

"Ms.," I corrected. "I'm not married. What are you calling for, Father Bible-Chapter?"

He coughed uncomfortably. "This might sound

strange, but… I believe you might be in danger."

Danger? Scratch that about my mood sinking. It was rising again. I was entertained more with everything he said. I stretched out languidly, settling in for a long, interesting phone call. He just *had* to start talking about how I was sinning and needed to atone for something, right? Oh, *boy*, if only he knew about Luce.

"I think you might have to elaborate just a little. Technically, everyone is in danger all of the time, don't you agree? Climate change and all that."

"Well, yes, I suppose that's true, but this is a more… specialized danger. An avoidable one. One that I am trained to combat."

Now images of priests fighting the sun with crucifixes popped into my head. Now there was a great idea for a terrible movie!

"Forgive me, Father, for I have sinned." The words had popped out of my mouth before I'd had a chance to think on them.

Silence.

Then, he cleared his throat. "Please, go on. I am here to listen."

Realistically speaking, what were the chances of a random priest calling me out of nowhere to take my confession? Because so far, he hadn't done an awful lot of trying to have me converted to whatever cult he belonged to and with a name like "Father Exodus," I sincerely doubted that he was an ordinary priest.

"Which congregation did you say you belonged to?" I asked.

"I am a member of the Ordo Sancti Matrem Suam."

Great. Latin. As far as I was concerned, that could mean absolutely anything.

"Well, Father Exodus, when I was four, I stuck a lollipop in my friend's hair."

"Is that all?" He sounded strained, as if he were trying to get me to say something else.

"Nope," I replied. "Everything else I've already been forgiven for, though, so that's all I got for you. But I don't think I need forgiveness from God for that if my friend's forgiven me, but hey, what do I know? After all, doesn't it say something like, 'Do as the heavens have done, forget your evil; With them forgive yourself'? Or something like that? Well, anyway, she got one stuck in my hair too, so I think it cancels out."

Hm, the heat was starting to get to me. My face was flushed, and I felt giddy, as well as a little dizzy. *I should probably get out of the bath soon.*

"I believe that was Shakespeare," Father Exodus said carefully.

I gasped dramatically. "Father! Don't tell me you read books other than the Bible? Isn't that some kind of sacrilege?"

He chuckled—I had actually made him chuckle.

It sounded nice, warm, and somehow, for just a moment, it gave me the fuzzies, though that could have just been the prolonged exposure to the heat of the bath.

"It is frowned upon, but will you keep my secret?" he asked.

I wished I had a face to match the voice. If he looked anything like he sounded, he was gorgeous, priest or not. Some members of the clergy could marry and have relationships, right? I wondered which kind he was. I didn't even know which religion he belonged to, though it was likely at least some variant of Christianity.

"I think I can do that," I promised. "As long as you put in a good word for my friend with the Big Guy."

He paused, but when he spoke again, the confusion in his tone was palpable. "You don't want me to put in a good word for *you*?"

My mind flashed to Luce, to Jonathan, to the deal I'd made. The one that had forfeited my soul. I'd known exactly what I was getting into. And I knew there was no way out of it. Not even the Devil himself could go back on a deal he'd made.

"No," I said quietly. "I don't."

I hung up.

I put my phone down on the stool beside the bath and sunk into the water, fully immersing my head. I stayed down there for half a minute, at least.

Listening to my thumping heartbeat that sounded like knocks on the roof, my eyes closed from the burning heat, I allowed my thoughts to run their course. I didn't focus on them, didn't try to control or direct them. I just let them do their thing until nothing but tranquility was left. Tranquility that was quickly replaced by the ardent desire and need to breathe.

Gasping for air, I broke the surface again. Okay. Time to get out for real. I also just realized that I had completely forgotten about the tea I'd made. What a waste. It would be completely cold now. And since it had been brewing this entire time, also painfully bitter.

Feeling exhausted and sluggish from the heat, I only just managed to drag myself to my bedroom wearing my towel and dropped onto my cool featherbed. I could stand to take a nap now.

"That does *not* look like you're ready," Luce commented dryly when I regained consciousness and found him standing over me, his arms crossed, and an eyebrow raised. He was ready to go out in his white shirt, the top three buttons left open to expose a delicate gold chain on his brown chest. His short, black hair was styled tastefully, and his chiseled abdomen was inferred by his tight clothing.

Groggy as I was feeling, I only groaned.

"Ames, I don't care what you look like, but we *are* going out tonight. So if you don't want to find yourself in a bar wearing nothing but this piece of damp cloth, I suggest you get a move on and put on some real clothes."

He needn't say more. Luce never made empty threats. He *would* transport me as I was if I didn't move, and I had no desire to take a role in that play. In record time, I threw on a black lace dress and painted my face—only the eyes and mouth, as I couldn't care less about foundation. Far too much effort. After giving my still-damp hair a quick brush and donning shoes and earrings, I breathlessly turned to Luce. "Ready."

He smirked and clicked his fingers. The same instant, we found ourselves in a moving limousine, though I was in no condition to appreciate it. My stomach was turning over, shocked by the sudden location change.

"Could you not?" I growled as I was squeezing my eyes shut and breathing in deeply to still the feelings of motion sickness.

"It's the fastest way to travel," he said, unfazed. "And the most convenient."

"Well, at least give me a warning next time." I glowered at him, even though I knew I really should have seen it coming.

"Here, have this," he said unaffectedly, handing

me a martini glass, complete with olive that had been sitting ready beside him. Disgruntled, despite the sickness fading, I took it, and cheered with him before gulping down basically the whole glass. The alcohol woke me up a little and took me out of my groggy misery. This was what I had asked for when I'd suggested going for drinks. Kind of.

I glanced out the windows of the limousine, watching the city lights flash by. No matter how often Luce took me out, I was still amazed by how he managed to avoid the traffic and get anywhere fast—even without using his translocation mojo. As for how he could afford to travel in as much style as he did—I thought it best not to ask. I had a feeling it wasn't a good idea to stick my nose too deep in the Devil's business. All I knew was that the vehicle was usually driven by someone who'd either made a deal with him, or someone from Hell who was trying to crawl up his ass.

"Where are we headed?" I asked, trying to stay nonchalant. Going out for drinks with Luce could mean ending up anywhere from a biker bar to a high-end soirée—and he never warned me which it was ahead of time. Judging by the limousine, I was guessing that tonight was a high-class event.

"A new night club is opening downtown," he said, self-appreciatively placing a hand on his hip. When he saw my displeased grimace, he added, "It's the new playground for the rich and famous. Trust me, it'll be fun."

I groaned, but I didn't try to change his mind.

Before long, the car stopped, and Luce got out, before offering me his hand for help. I took it gratefully, and only a moment later, I was blinded by flashing lights. Photographers blasted at us from all sides, and there was actually a red carpet in front of us. A red carpet that Luce led me down, strolling, all confidence, not even so much as blinking in the direction of the cameras. A reporter came up to us, but Luce only smiled at her, and she veered away, as if she'd never seen us in the first place. He waved his hand, and suddenly, all the cameras stopped flashing us and the operators veered away to focus their attention on something else. I wasn't worried about the photographs. Luce had his powers.

"Someday, you'll have to teach me how to do that," I muttered under my breath.

He flashed me a grin. "No way. I've gotta keep my secrets."

We got to the end of the carpet and the doorman—a hefty white guy wearing a black suit and sunglasses—let us in without so much as a pause. Again—this was no longer something I questioned. The Devil had his ways.

The inside of the club was already filled with people. And so it was unsurprising that I lost sight of Luce the second I let go of his arm. Not having any money or my phone with me, there wasn't much I could do in a club like this. Well, except for the obvious. I made my way to the dance floor and joined the thrashing masses—significantly less crowded than in a common club and significantly better dressed, but the rest was more or less the same. Women were throwing themselves at men, men were grinding up on women, and any conversation took place in the smoking area because that was the only place where you could hear yourself think.

I enjoyed dancing. I used to be in a troupe, and we'd been good—like, really good. We'd had shows all over the place. But then I had grown up and had to get a job and pay taxes and take out insurance and all those little fun hobbies that young people got to have... I didn't have the time or money for them anymore. Never even mind the energy. I had dropped it when I'd been with Jonathan, specifically so I could spend more time with him. It was times like these when I remembered how much I enjoyed dancing. How much I missed it.

It really didn't take long before my pure enjoyment was ruined. I could feel some guy dance up behind me, getting far too close to my body for comfort. I ignored it, but after only another moment, his surprisingly small hands were on my hips. I didn't hesitate to turn around and flick him in the forehead, even though I had to stand on my toes to reach. He stumbled back, his perfectly sculpted black eyebrows raised in surprise, and I used the opportunity to disappear into the crowd again. He'd been some actor who'd recently gotten his big break in a Hollywood blockbuster. Still new to the big leagues though. I recognized a lot of faces around the club when I actually looked at the people, but it really didn't mean very much to me. Five years ago, I would have been awe-struck. Funny how being friends with the Devil put things in perspective.

Speaking of the Devil, there he was, weaving through the crowd with two filled glasses in hand. He had no trouble finding me and handed me one of them.

"See anything you like?" he asked. Here was another thing about him. Despite my ears being literally deafened by the blasting speakers, I could hear and understand him without having to strain myself.

I raised an eyebrow. "Hardly," I said. I didn't bother shouting, knowing that he'd hear me just fine.

He shrugged, and we knocked back our drinks. He took my glass again and somehow made both of them vanish, before dragging me back onto the dance floor. As we danced, I started noticing a circle forming around us, people watching in awe and cheering us on. Another fact about the Devil: He was one hell of a dancer. Even as we spun around, I could see the gazes of many women and men alike glued to him, some even biting their lips. He didn't care. Luce wasn't here to seduce, he was here with me, having fun as my friend.

After a little while, that actor from before infiltrated the circle, pushing to swap in for Luce. Clearly hoping to give me the opportunity to get laid like any good wingman, Luce tried to respectfully bow out, but I grabbed his sleeve and followed him.

"Can we go somewhere calmer?" I asked, and he obliged, grinning. He snapped his fingers, and, with another flash of sickness, we sat in a quiet bar, some sort of cocktail bar by the looks of it. This time, I'd been prepared for the motion sickness, and as soon as it passed, I sighed in relief. Luce had already vanished to get us drinks again and I closed my eyes, relishing the peaceful, quiet jazz music in the background. The place was by no means empty, but it was laid out in a fashion that meant that didn't matter.

"How was the fitting?" Luce asked when he came back and set a Sex on the Beach down in front of me.

"I found her the perfect dress," I admitted, smiling wistfully at the memory of Lynn crying with happiness. It hadn't just been about the dress, I knew. It had been about wearing the dress when she would swear her everlasting love to Taylor. It had been about her future happiness. Maybe, if it could lead to something like that, trying again to find someone might not be so bad.

I set my gaze on Luce, determined to move

forward. "About what you said yesterday," I said, but I stopped myself. While it hadn't been the first time Luce had made that offer, I really had no way of knowing how serious he'd actually been.

Still, his eyes lit up and his smirk widened. "I get to set you up, don't I?"

Looking at his sparkling eyes, I hesitated. This was a terrible idea, wasn't it? "First, why do you want to do that, anyway?"

"Easy. I can't undo the past, but I still think you deserve happiness. Besides, if I have to drag you to Hell anyway, wouldn't it be so much better if you had a reason for happiness there already? If you date one of my buddies, then the transition would be much easier, and it would make it more natural for us to keep hanging out after you die."

He spoke so cheerfully about my demise, it made it seem like it just wasn't a big deal at all. It almost made me think that dying wouldn't matter too much. Almost.

His reasoning was as sound as any argument I could expect to get out of him.

"So?" he prodded, watching me meaningfully.

"Fine," I sighed, desperately hoping I wasn't going to regret this. "Just don't go mushy on me, okay? You can set me up with one of your buddies from Hell. I need a date to Lynn's wedding anyway."

Chapter 9

Sunday mornings might have just been my favorite thing in the world. The knowledge that I didn't have to do *anything* all day, that I had no obligations because no one would want anything from me, either, gave me such an immense sense of freedom and bliss that waking up in bed to the tentative rays of the morning sun peeking through my curtains was nothing short of perfection. Content with my situation, I snuggled deeper into the covers, my dreams still half-lingering in my consciousness.

Too bad my peace and quiet was rudely interrupted by my ringing phone. Instantly annoyed, I glanced at it, only to see Lynn's name displayed. *Ugh, fine.* If it had been anyone else, I'd have ignored it, but she *had* just made me her maid of honor.

"Hngh?" I answered lazily.

"Don't tell me you're still asleep?" She sounded unnecessarily chipper. Far too awake for a sane person on a Sunday morning.

"Nghu." Non-committal noises were all she was going to get from me if she insisted on calling so early.

"It's already past nine A.M.! Come on, you've got to get up and start the day!"

Exactly. Not even ten o'clock yet. On a *Sunday*. And I had a tradition of spending my Sunday mornings in very close quarters with my bed. It was kind of a long-term commitment.

"Blugh."

"Well, anyway, I wanted to talk to you about all the maid of honor stuff, and I figured better sooner than later. So how about I come by this afternoon? I'll bring burritos, extra spicy!"

At the sound of extra-spicy burritos, I finally perked up a little. "Yum?"

"Yes, yum yum." Lynn laughed. "Let's make it lunch."

"Mhm," I said, yawning heartily.

"See you later!"

She hung up and I cuddled back into my downs. But not for long. A sudden whiff of rotten eggs announced that my nap time had officially ended. Still, I refused to accept it. I squeezed my eyes shut, intent on ignoring anything and anyone, but when Luce threw open my bedroom doors, even I couldn't keep pretending.

"Wakey-wakey, eggs and bakey," he sang, pulling the covers off me. I pulled my knees up and glared at him, but he remained unaffected. I hated how perfect he looked first thing in the morning. Even now, he was wearing his usual pristinely ironed shirt and jeans, his hair impeccably styled. "I got you a date for tonight."

Never mind the sleep. I instantly shot up, wide awake. "You got me a what now?"

"A date," he repeated, giving me his most winning smile. The one that could melt icebergs and save the *Titanic* from sinking. "Let me tell you more over coffee."

He pranced downstairs and I trudged after him sullenly.

"Tea," I grumbled. "Don't you dare bring that nasty brew near me."

I took a seat at the kitchen isle, letting him deal with the drink preparations. I watched him bustle about in silence, still annoyed at my weekly sleep-in having been cut short by everyone in my life conspiring against me, and tried to figure out how my Sundays had suddenly become so hectic. Could I potentially back out of one of my newly gained commitments? Starting with this date thing?

"Talk," I ordered when Luce finally handed over my mug with steaming Earl Grey.

"He's a King of Hell—you could consider him my cousin, if you like. He was one of the angels who followed me when I was cast from Heaven and all that—which means he's an advocate for free speech and choice—and he can really be quite charming."

Processing the information, I squinted at him, neatly filing every piece of information in the right place in my head.

"But?" I asked. There was always a *but*. And if Luce didn't mention it now, that meant that it was something all the worse.

"But nothing," he replied earnestly. "He was one of the first to take my side. If anything, he can be a little intense." He laughed. "You could say he's loyal to a fault. And isn't that exactly what you need?"

He wasn't entirely wrong. Loyalty and commitment—these were the two things that had become most important to me in the last few years.

"What's his name?"

"It's Paimon. But on Earth, he usually goes by Cornelius."

"Cornelius?" I echoed with a raised eyebrow. "Really?"

It wasn't that unusual for demons to go by aliases when dealing with humans, according to Luce, but usually, they stayed to something that was closer to their real names, at least.

"I know." Luce sighed. "He's always liked to give his imagination more freedom, I suppose. In any case—he'll pick you up for dinner at seven."

"Wow, wait!" Holding up my hands to slow him down, I took a deep breath, trying to force oxygen to my brain so my cells would work quicker. It was still too early. The tea wasn't helping enough. "How did you even set this up so fast?"

Suddenly, Luce wasn't meeting my gaze anymore.

Instead, he found a lot of interest in the ceiling fan.

"Luce?" I warned.

I pinned him down with my gaze, staring until he finally relented.

"He may have expressed interest in meeting you in the past," he admitted. "And it may not have been completely unrelated to things I said about you."

"I don't even want to know." I groaned, sinking down in my chair until my head was resting on my crossed arms atop the counter. "Just so I know what I'm getting into — is he also fond of that translocation thing you do?"

Luce chuckled. "I told him you didn't like it, so I think he'll figure out another mode of transportation. Don't worry, it'll be fine. He's not that different to me."

I shot him a side-long glance. "That's what I'm worried about."

By the time Lynn came around carrying delicious… ahem… breakfast burritos, Luce was still talking to me about potential dates. It turned out, not only had he set me up with his buddy, oh no, he had enlisted *all* of the Kings and Dukes of Hell to go on dates with me if I didn't like Paimon. Clearly, he *really* wanted me to date one of them. Not for the first time, I wondered why Luce had decided to befriend me instead of just waiting quietly to harvest my soul. And why he was making such a big effort to keep me around, trying to find a way to make sure I'd be happy and comfortable in Hell, as odd and contradictory as it sounded.

He was in the middle of telling me about Asmodeus's best qualities and probing my willingness to engage in polyamory when I opened the door for Lynn.

Luce stopped himself midsentence and swept toward her.

"Lynn, how wonderful to see you!" He picked her up and twirled her around once before setting her down again. Miraculously, she didn't drop her precious food cargo. A flustered smile appeared on her lips.

"Lucian," she said, a hint of crimson coming to her cheeks. "It's been a while."

"Too long, my dear. Too long."

I observed the interaction cautiously, moving between the two to prevent any bad ideas from hatching. I hadn't forgotten how they'd almost become a couple a few years back, just before Lynn and Taylor had found each other. And clearly, Lynn hadn't forgotten either. But I knew how much she loved Taylor, and I equally knew how *tempting* the Devil could be. I didn't want to risk having her succumb to that. The worst part was—he wasn't even doing it on purpose.

"Tea?" I asked, hoping to break the tension. "Water? Juice? Soda?"

Somehow, I managed to peel Lynn's eyes from Luce. "Sparkling water, please."

She was the only person I knew who liked the stuff, but for her sake, I always had a few bottles in the house. Just before I went to grab it, I turned to Luce, glaring at him meaningfully. "Luce? Don't forget you had that thing. Remember?"

I raised an eyebrow, hoping that was enough for him to get the message. It was. Unfortunately, he decided to ignore it. He smiled back at me, as innocently as a crocodile.

"Oh, don't worry, I canceled. I wouldn't want to miss out on all the fun with my two favorite ladies, after all."

I groaned, but I let them be, hoping I could trust them to keep their hands to themselves. Seeing as Luce was by nature someone who respected choice, he wouldn't be forcing anything if she wasn't up for it and Lynn wouldn't start anything to jeopardize her relationship, of that much at least I could be certain. Probably.

Nevertheless, I hurried, refusing to tempt the fates and allow even the slightest chance for a mishap that could destroy my friend's happiness. Luckily, when I got back from the basement, they were still chatting easily, doing no more than catching up on what had happened since they'd last seen each other. I left them to it just a little longer while I set out some cake from the freezer to let it thaw. We'd want that later, there was no doubt about it. Since it didn't seem like Luce was planning to go anywhere, I'd included him in the count for slices.

"So, where do we start?" I took a seat, facing Lynn across the kitchen isle, tapping a pen against a notebook I'd set out earlier.

"Oh, is this a bridesmaid talk?" Luce asked, his eyes sparkling. "How exciting!"

I wanted to roll my eyes at him, but frankly, I was getting a little excited about the idea as well. I'd always thought it would be cool to be a maid of honor. It was a weird low-key dream of mine—I'd wanted it more than even being a bride—at least before I'd met Jonathan. And after, as well. I mean, come on, getting to be a big part of what might be the happiest day in my best friend's life and seeing her face light up in bliss from the best seats in the house? Sign me up!

"So, where do we start?" I repeated. "What do you need me to take care of?"

Lynn gave Luce one last coquettish glance before she returned to reality and me. After rummaging around in her purse, she pulled out her phone and found a list she'd made on it.

"I need you to come to the cake testing with me— Taylor won't be able to make it because of work. So I figured we could choose the best three and bring slices of them home to her so she can have the final pick."

"When is it?" I asked, wandering over to my calendar on the wall.

"The week after next, on Wednesday afternoon. We can move it to the evening if you can't go at three because of work."

I contemplated the luxury of taking a half day for the sake of cake and my best friend. "No way. Three it is. I'll be there."

In the worst-case scenario, I'd pretend to be sick. But I should have enough extra hours saved up that taking a half day should absolutely not be an issue. Never mind that I still had vacation days waiting for me to pencil them in. I scribbled the appointment into the calendar in red, marking it with highlighter, to ensure there was no way I could forget.

"What else?" I whipped back around to her.

"I have a dress now, but we need to find you guys bridesmaid dresses. I wanted your input on that as well."

"Oh, can I help with that?" Luce chimed in. He almost looked like a small child, begging to be allowed to play.

"Are you sure?" Lynn pretended to be hesitant, but I could see that she was rearing to say *yes*. To be fair, with Luce's sense of style, not much could go wrong.

"I think that's a good idea," I said. "Do you have

pictures of the others so he can start thinking about it?"

Lynn nodded and flipped through her phone to find a photo of Brianna.

"Hailey is going to be Taylor's bridesmaid now, by the way, so it'll just be you and Bri for me," Lynn said to me while Luce inspected Brianna's picture earnestly.

He nodded after he had memorized the biggest details about her looks. "What about your dress?" he then asked, just as Lynn was about to put the phone away. She blushed and threw me an uncertain glance. I raised an eyebrow. "It's not *him* you're marrying."

That was all I needed to say. She pulled up a photo of her in the dress she'd asked me to take yesterday, once we had all gotten over our initial overwhelmed state.

Luce whistled through his teeth.

"Not bad at all! And *you* picked that?" He glanced at me with an appraising gaze.

I crossed my arms, narrowing my eyes at him. "No need to sound so surprised, you know. I managed my own wardrobe just fine before you showed up."

I must have been glaring daggers because he raised his hands in defense and chuckled. "Okay, I hear you. I just never pegged you as someone who'd be good at choosing wedding dresses. You're more the casual-style type, if you know what I mean?"

I looked down at my outfit—a grey tank top underneath a red-and-black checkered open flannel shirt and ordinary blue jeans. "Not really?"

He sighed. "It's a good choice is what I'm saying. Just not really your usual style."

Well, I couldn't deny that. I wasn't exactly in the habit of picking out wedding dresses every other day, after all.

Seeing that he had appeased me for the moment, Luce turned his attention back to the picture of the wedding dress and rubbed his stubbly beard. "We'll need dresses that match the elegance but have more muted colors so you stand out more..." His eyes whipped up to us, his gaze and tone determined. "Silver," he said. "Or a light grey with sparkly accents. Simple, straight-lined dresses reminiscent of ancient Greece."

Lynn and I looked at one another, both grinning as we imagined his idea. It was perfect.

"Guess we can put a tick on that part of the list." I said before turning back to Luce. "But you *are* going to come to the store with us to pick out the right dresses, you hear me?"

He took a cheeky overplayed bow. "Whatever your heart desires—I am but your humble servant."

"Oh, please." Lynn elbowed me. "You just want a buffer between you and the others."

I shrugged. "It might be nice having someone not

glaring at me the entire time, that's all I'm saying. Glaring is normally my job."

"And might I add, you are getting better at it every day." Luce chimed in cheerfully, which warranted him a sharp look from me. But then we all broke into laughter.

Suddenly, I realized that I hadn't eaten yet all day, and that the burritos were still sitting untouched in their aluminum wrapping on the table, so I snatched one up and stuffed the first bite of the delicious, fiery spice wrap into my mouth.

"Got an appointment for that?" I asked between bites.

Lynn donated her burrito to Luce, who loved spicy food almost as much as I did, before answering. "You should already have that marked in your calendar, you know? It's Saturday, same time as yesterday."

That did ring a bell. I checked the calendar, cursing myself for not having entered the appointment before. I guessed that getting Lynn's dress had just taken complete priority in my mind and I'd forgotten about mine and those of the other women. I entered it now, with three red exclamation marks.

"Which reminds me," Lynn continued, "could you… go to Taylor's fitting as well? Just so someone who knows my dress is there to stop any big color clashes…?"

I frowned. "Isn't her sister going to be there?"

Lynn bit her lip, looking away. "Yeah, she will, but Hailey… She's a bit…"

"Say no more." I remembered full well what dress she'd picked out for Lynn. There was a high chance she'd do the same for her sister. "When?"

"Ooh, can I help?" Luce chimed in before Lynn had a chance to answer. He was almost bouncing on the spot.

I knew Lynn and I had the same thought the moment our gazes met. Having Luce choose Taylor's dress would be *perfect*. Thanks to the photo, he knew what Lynn's dress looked like, and neither of us would ever doubt his impeccable taste. Plus, it meant that I didn't need to sacrifice another day, though I'd do it in a heartbeat if Lynn asked.

"Please do." Lynn said, clasping his hands. "Thank you so much, Lucian!"

I took my calendar off the wall and slapped it on the table in front of Lynn.

"To fulfill my maid-of-honor duties properly, I'm going to need you to tell me which weekends you're available and without responsibilities, *chica*." I didn't need to tell her it was for the bachelorette party. Lynn always knew what I meant. Watching her leaf through the pages, marking several weekends between now and the wedding only three months from now, I added, "I also want to know what your limits are."

"Limits?" Her eyes shot up to me, along with an eyebrow.

"Yeah. What's off-limits? And if there's a direction you want me to go in, you better let me know now."

Lynn sighed and pushed the calendar back over to me.

"Just don't get me a stripper. And be sure to be imaginative." She smirked at me. "I'm sure you can think up something good."

"Just you, me, and Brianna?"

Luce looked up mid-bite, hurt written all over his face. "What about me?"

I rolled my eyes. "Are you a bridesmaid?"

Lynn coughed uncomfortably and shot me an apologetic glance before turning to him.

"Actually, I was going to ask if you'd like to take Hailey's spot…? We don't have a groom, but you could be my… uh… bridesman?"

Luce beamed at her, all charm and no decency as he took her hand and blew a kiss on it.

"It would be my pleasure." Then he directed his widest grin at me. I could only shake my head at him. He'd won. He always won.

I gave him my most sickeningly-sweet smile. "I guess you better get in shape for your silver Greek-style dress, *Lucy.*"

Chapter 5

Lynn's list was long, but we managed to tick off everything and send her on her way home in time for me to get ready for my date with a demon. Her relatively speedy departure was aided by Luce whispering the secret to her when he thought I couldn't hear—well, half of the secret. Lynn still remained blissfully unaware of Luce's real identity, after all, and of factual proof that Hell was an actual place that existed. Though, as it turned out, the Bible had still gotten most things wrong. Not surprising, considering it had been written by human men, not an angel or anything of the sort.

"Not that dress," Luce argued against my choice of wardrobe.

"Why not?" I turned in the mirror, looking at myself, letting the thigh-length turquoise skirt swish with a little spin. It was a fine dress, not too flashy, not too showy, not too prude… Elegant and cheeky, the way I liked it. The halter neck bodice accentuated both my breasts and back, and the asymmetrical skirt and waistline didn't draw attention to the "little extra" on my hips that I felt self-conscious about.

Plus, it had pockets. And let's face it—any dress with pockets gained some serious brownie points.

"It doesn't exactly say: I look forward to this date but will kick your ass if you touch me without consent. And trust me, that's what you want your outfit to be saying tonight."

I glanced at Luce, suddenly feeling a little apprehensive about this plan of his. What exactly had I agreed to by going on a date with Paimon? Hadn't there been something said about Paimon respecting my choices…?

"Fine." I shrugged, giving in. "Since you're clearly trying to look out for me, why don't you pick my outfit?"

I dropped on my bed as he rubbed his hands together gleefully. "I thought you'd never ask. I'll be right back."

I blinked, and he was gone, leaving behind the smell of rotten eggs. Exasperated yet to equal parts resigned, I grabbed the air freshener I kept on the bedside table and tried to overpower the stench with lavender. When that didn't entirely work, I gave in and opened the window fully, even though it was permanently cracked open either way.

It was quiet outside, and while it wasn't dark yet, you could feel that evening was fast approaching. A movement caught my eye from the corner of my vision, near the bushes in my front garden, but when I focused in on it, I couldn't make out anything out of the ordinary. Then, suddenly, a little black bird fled a bush and took to the sky. Slowly, I let my gaze wander across the garden and down the street. There weren't many cars there and most I recognized. Though when my eyes travelled to the end of the street, I noticed a car backing away from the corner, just a little. Weird. I couldn't fully explain it, but something didn't feel quite right.

A sudden rush of adrenaline induced the feeling of anticipation, of an oncoming storm, and I held my breath for just a moment. But the sky, while not exactly clear, didn't even show signs of rain, never mind a storm. Even though I tried to rationalize it to myself—that I'd just been startled by a bird taking flight and my body was trying to trick me into fight-or-flight mode, I couldn't shake off the bad feeling. For the first time in probably ever, I closed the window when it was neither cold, nor raining, nor windy.

"All right, now what do you say about this?" Luce's sudden arrival, along with the usual smell, startled me more than it had since he'd done it the first time. An actual squeak escaped my lips and I flinched, whirling around to him. He froze.

"Ames, are you okay?" He lowered the hanger he'd been holding up and crossed over to me, peering in my face with an expression that spoke only of concern. "You're so pale… What happened?"

Suddenly, the absurdity of my irrational fear

overcame me, and I burst into laughter. I was acting so silly. "Nothing. It's all good, I just… scared myself, I guess. Now show me what you've got."

His easy grin returning to his face, he held up the hanger again. All right! It was classy yet gave off the kind of ass-kicking vibe he had mentioned.

"I can work with this," I smirked, before shedding the dress I was wearing and donning the black pants, the grey shirt with a beautifully stitched, low-cut V-neckline, and the leather jacket that completed the outfit. I had just the boots to finish the outfit off sitting downstairs, calling my name.

"Not bad," I said when I looked at myself in the mirror. It even worked with the makeup I was already wearing—one less thing to worry about. Everything fit perfectly, undoubtedly thanks to Luce's Hell or angel powers. If he'd been a character in a movie or a TV show, I'd be annoyed at how universally overpowered he seemed. But as his friend… It certainly had its upsides. Besides, he wasn't without his flaws, either.

"Well…" He said, arching an eyebrow. "Paimon will be here any second now, so I think it's time for me to leave."

And with that, he was gone, leaving behind the stench of rotten eggs once again. Coughing to alleviate the burn in my lungs, I opened the window again before grabbing my inhaler from my bedside table and taking a hit. Then I wandered downstairs and let the inhaler fall into my purse, wondering where Paimon was going to take me.

Once again, I questioned my sanity for agreeing to date a demon, but then again, the train to save my sanity had long left the station. I waited, sitting at the kitchen isle, flicking through my bridesmaid notes absentmindedly.

The doorbell and my phone rang almost simultaneously. Seeing that my phone was once again only presenting me with a withheld number, I opted for just opening the door instead.

I sincerely hoped the dreamboat standing there in a dapper suit was my date because if he wasn't, I was going to invite him in for a nightcap and ditch Paimon altogether. He had the same dark complexion Luce sported, deep, dark eyes that appeared almost black, a fashionable, short haircut along with a clean shave to show off his chiseled jaw and cheekbones, and a smoldering look in his eye. Even his aftershave was intoxicating.

"Hi," he said, his voice silky-smooth with the smallest Eastern accent. "You must be Amelia. It's nice to meet you. I'm Cornelius."

I just about managed to take his outstretched hand, shaking it slowly, before I realized I was staring and caught myself.

"Nice to meet you too," I said, feeling a little embarrassed about how quickly he'd taken me off guard. I shouldn't have been surprised he was handsome. Luce was nothing to sniff at, either, after all. Why should a fellow fallen angel be anything else?

"Shall we?" His smile and inviting gesture were almost too much. It was charming; it was dashing; it was like I was on a date with a guy from my naughty dreams, making me wonder how far Paimon would be willing to go with a human. I hoped he wasn't just going on this date to appeal to Luce, or to do him a favor. Who knew if Luce had exaggerated when he'd mentioned Paimon's interest in meeting me?

Paimon led me to his car—a slick, black Mercedes—and even opened the door to the passenger seat for me before getting behind the wheel himself.

Ordinarily, I had a rule about first dates that included driving myself to the destination in my own car and meeting my date there, but that would have been pointless with Paimon. He likely had similar powers to Luce's, after all. And honestly, I found the experience thrilling. Not knowing where we were going, not having to worry about traffic, about being on time, about how I would recognize my date… It was freeing and equally kind of exciting. As he put the car into drive, Paimon's eyes flicked over to me, an intensity in the gaze I hadn't expected so early on in the night.

"You're beautiful" —my heart skipped a beat— "for a human."

Those last three words left a bitter taste in my mouth and alarm bells started ringing all around my head.

"I look forward to finding out why Lord Lucifer treasures you." His eyes softened when he mentioned Luce, and he averted his gaze to focus on driving.

Swallowing hard, I tried to rationalize his words in my head. He was an angel-slash-demon who only wore a human disguise. It was no surprise that they might have different beauty standards. But then again, could Paimon even appreciate human aesthetics? Did he understand them? Had he said it because he meant it or because he thought it was the right thing to say?

Even though I knew I was overanalyzing the situation, I had nothing else to do for the entirety of the drive, as Paimon didn't seem interested in conversing while driving just yet. Admittedly, I didn't mind too much. I didn't want to say anything I would regret, and I always felt weird talking to someone who didn't look me in the eyes. And if he *had* looked me in the eyes, I'd be a lot more concerned about my safety, because that would mean he wasn't looking at the road. Safety first. Romance later. Then again, if I died now and went to Hell, we could probably just pick up the date there. I couldn't deny that dying would put a significant damper on our relationship, though. I liked being alive and had no intention to change that state quite so soon.

Finally, we arrived at our destination—a parking lot in a well-off area I rarely found reason to visit—and I'd made the decision to forgive him for his earlier comment, telling myself that he had probably not meant it as callously as it had felt to me in that moment.

Before I even had the chance to loosen my seatbelt, Paimon had somehow come around to the other side of the car and opened the door for me, offering me his hand to help me out.

"Thanks," I said.

"Don't mention it." His smile was radiant. "Lord Lucifer told me that dining is a common activity for a first date here. I hope that's all right with you."

"That sounds perfect."

His statement told me one of two things: Either this was the first time he'd gone on a date with a human woman, or he wanted me to believe that was the case. Either way, I was willing to give him the benefit of the doubt.

I followed him around the corner to a restaurant— a fancy one with someone standing at the entrance with an oversized book to check reservations—where we were seated as soon as he told the maître d' his fake human name. We were guided to our table beside a large window facing the waterfront. I had to admit, Paimon had chosen well. *Extremely* well. I wasn't sure I'd ever been in a similarly fancy situation with anyone but Luce and I was beginning to feel underdressed.

Once we were settled at our table, and had both given our order to our waiter, the serious part of the date began.

"Amelia," he said, that dazzling smile on display again, "let me be frank with you."

I looked back at him earnestly. The air was sizzling with anticipation, with electricity that I couldn't quite gauge.

"I have been wanting to meet you for quite some time now. You have awakened my curiosity, which, I assure you, is no simple feat. I'm certain you will not disappoint me." There was a dark quality to his tone and gaze, almost as if he were appraising my worth, warning me about what he might do if I did not meet his expectations.

"Why is that?" I asked, my voice steady, certain. His charm and charisma might have taken me by surprise, but his veiled threat left me cold and unafraid.

Our drinks came, a gin and tonic for me, a bloody mary for him, along with glasses of water.

"Because you have captured Lord Lucifer's attention," Paimon explained, stirring his drink slowly, after the waiter had left. "You were meant to be just another human he made a deal with, but for some reason, he gives you special attention, and I want to know why."

I couldn't blame him for being curious. I had wondered often enough as well, without ever arriving at an answer, but I had a feeling Paimon wouldn't be satisfied if I told him that.

Backstory time, I supposed. I sighed.

"My fiancé was in a coma because of a bad car crash. I was desperate, and I would have done anything to save him because it was looking like he wouldn't wake back up again. The doctors said only a miracle would save him. That's when Luce showed up."

"'*Luce*'?" The aghast tone and wide eyes told me that in Paimon's eyes, I had just severely insulted his master's honor by shortening his name. But Luce didn't care, and neither did I.

"Yes, Luce." I gave Paimon a stern look for interrupting me and continued. "He made a deal with me: My soul in exchange for Jonathan's life."

Paimon nodded, leaning forward to catch every word that tumbled from my lips. This upcoming part was the bit he wanted to know. I supposed everything else was pretty standard for a day in Hell.

"*Jonathan*," I said, extending his name with emphasis, "decided it would be a great idea to sleep around basically as soon as he was discharged from the hospital, though. So after I found him in *my* bed with someone else, I kicked him out and set fire to the bed. In the back yard, of course. While it was burning, Luce showed up again, we had a talk, some drinks, and since then, he keeps coming back to raid my fridge and drinks cabinet. And that's my relationship to Luce in a nutshell. Satisfied?"

Paimon stared at me, the gears in his mind ticking away. His gaze turned dark as he looked me up and down. His lips moved, but no sound came out. Patiently waiting for him to catch himself, I took a few sips of my gin and tonic. Meanwhile, he ruffled his hair in exasperation, shaking his head over and over again, before finally slamming both fists down on the table so hard, it made the cutlery jump.

"No!" he yelped. The restaurant continued as if nothing had happened, as if no one had noticed his outburst. And, glancing around, I realized they hadn't. No one was even looking our way. Paimon must have used some sort of angel or demon magic to prevent anyone from listening in on our private not-very-date-like chat. Or else everyone here was just *very* polite. This conversation was turning more into an interrogation than anything else. "Why? Why is he wasting his time with you? You don't matter! You're just a human!"

"Oh, gee, thanks," I said. "Sorry to burst your bubble, but that's really all there is to it. I guess he just likes spending time with me." I shrugged. "Maybe he was sick of being put on a pedestal by people… er, sorry, demons, like you."

That shut him up. For a moment. Then he shook his head again before studying me intently. "No, that's not it. He is above such things. There has to be another reason. But apparently, it's something you are unaware of."

I wasn't surprised that he didn't even consider the possibility that I might be lying. Luce had told me before—humans were incapable of lying to an angel, fallen or otherwise. I'd put it to the test before, too. Small things that weren't really lies, like minor omissions and sarcasm, those didn't seem to count. But intentional lying just... wasn't possible. It was like the presence of an angel compelled me to tell the truth. Which was why I never played poker with Luce. Or did any other kind of gambling when he was around.

"You really look up to him, don't you?" I said, tilting my head. I wondered for how long he'd been badgering Luce to let him meet me so he could get the answers to the questions that vexed him.

Paimon nodded, looking somewhat dejected. "He opened my eyes to the world, showed me what we could be, how we could be more. If not for him, I could never have asked such a simple question: *Why.* It holds power, that word. He guided me, all of us, and all of humanity, into a new future, one that we could shape ourselves."

I couldn't help but notice how his eyes brightened again when he spoke about Luce. And how much like a preacher he sounded. Made me wonder if he was secretly the founder of Satanism. He certainly was a Devil-stan.

Even though Paimon was a bit too fanatic for my liking, I could understand where he was coming from. The way I saw it, Luce had done a lot of good for humans too, by supporting our freedom of will, free choice and all that, depending on how true the stories were. Somehow, I'd never really wanted to ask Luce about what religious views were true, and what had truly happened, though I'd picked up a lot of things just by spending time with him and taking in offhand remarks of his. In the same vein, I had never asked him about Hell and what it was like. I'd find out soon enough, after all. No point in fretting ahead of time. I could neither change it, nor prepare for it.

Our food arrived, and our conversation came to a lull for the moment as we both focused our attention on eating. After I had stilled my initial hunger and satisfied my biggest cravings, I looked up to find Paimon eating slowly, very deliberately, almost as though it were a chore.

"Does it taste all right?" I asked. He looked at me, his eyebrows twitching, lines marring his forehead for just a moment, and then looked down at the food on his fork.

"I," He began, but he trailed off as confusion spread across his face. "I really don't know."

I set down my own fork. "If you like, we can go somewhere else, do something different. We don't have to have dinner, you know."

He contemplated my offer for a moment before nodding. "All right. Come with me."

Leaving several bills on the table, he rose from his seat, offering his hand. I took it, grabbing my purse with my other hand, and allowed him to lead me out of the restaurant. It was dark out now, and this part of the city had gone quieter. I expected Paimon to go back to the car, but instead, he led me down different roads until we reached a park. The gate had been closed already, locked and all, but with a snap of his fingers, Paimon opened it and led me through.

"Where are we going?"

He didn't respond. Instead, he led me farther toward the park's center, past bushes and trees and benches.

"You can just take me home if you prefer. You don't have to spend the evening with me. You got the information you were looking for, didn't you? I've told you pretty much everything I've got."

At this, he stopped and turned to me. Even though it was dark, there was a faint, flickering glow behind his eyes, imbuing them with an intensity I had rarely before seen.

"No," he said. "My mission has not changed. I need to know why Lord Lucifer stays by your side. And since you don't know, I will just have to find out on my own—by spending time with you as well."

I groaned inwardly. A part of me had hoped I

could just go home and sleep, so I'd be well-rested for work tomorrow, but hearing Paimon, that faint hint of desperation and confusion, I knew I had no choice. Somehow, understanding Luce's reason was of existential essence to him, and he would get no rest until he knew. What a pain.

I sighed. "So where are we going?"

His eyebrows knit together. "We're going on a walk through the park, obviously." He gestured at the trees. "That's what humans do on dates."

Pursing my lips, I contemplated his actions. He might know how the world worked in theory, but he had not interacted much with humans before, at least not socially, that much was becoming clear. Here he was, trying to imitate a romantic stroll by dragging me through a dark park at high speeds.

I wanted to explain to him how his actions were slightly unfitting, but my phone rang before I had the chance. I pulled it from my purse and picked up even before checking the screen. Anything to escape this conversation. "Yup?"

"Amelia?"

I recognized that voice, but I couldn't pinpoint it right away. "Uh... Yeah?"

"This is Father Exodus. We spoke yesterday."

"Um... hi." I glanced at Paimon, who was standing beside me, watching my actions closely, as though he were hoping to find some kind of sign in them.

"Sorry," I said. "I'm kind of busy right now, so…"

"Wait," Father Exodus said quickly. "I just… God granted me a… a vision, of sorts, and it was about you."

Weirdest pickup line I'd ever heard. "Uh-huh."

"And uh… Amelia, are you in any danger? It seems to me like… you might be being dragged by… demonic forces. Please, I can help."

Yup. Either this was the most bizarre scam I'd ever come across, or this priest was trying to convert me to join some form of weird sect. Then again. He wasn't exactly wrong. I certainly *was* being dragged around by demonic forces. I glanced around, on the off-chance I'd see some guy in robes sitting in the bushes somewhere nearby. Nothing. In a moment he'd probably ask me to pay him some money for an over-the-phone exorcism for the ghosts that haunted and plagued me. Genuinely wouldn't be the first time that had happened.

"I'm fine," I said, adding as much cheerfulness to my voice as I could. "I really don't think I'm in any danger."

Paimon was still watching me closely. It was honestly kind of embarrassing. I turned away from him to face the other way while I finished up the call. "But I've really got to go. There's someone waiting for me."

I hung up.

I'd enjoyed my call with Father Exodus yesterday,

but I really hadn't expected to ever hear from him again. Besides, it just struck me as weird that a random priest would call out of nowhere. That wasn't normal—right? But that was something to contemplate at a later point. Right now, a demon was waiting behind me.

Pensively, I stuck my phone back in my bag and turned to Paimon, only to find him standing in the same spot in what I assumed had to be his demon shape. His limbs were impossibly long and muscular, while his torso still retained the same size as his human body. Where he had worn a three-piece suit before, there were now scarves and colorful wrappings. Three thin but long tails weaved out behind him. His face had changed, too. His nose reminded me of a camel's, but his teeth looked like that of a carnivore—a wolf, perhaps. His long ears seemed distinctly canine as well, but his eyes retained the same look as before, including the light glow. Flames were flickering in them where the pupil should have been.

"Do you believe you're in danger now?" he asked, his voice booming and loud. I flinched at the sudden sound and rubbed my aching ears that felt as if he had shouted right into them.

"Not really." I groaned. "But that hurts. Mind using your inside voice?"

He took a step toward me, lifting a hand, which, I now saw, had long, razor-sharp claws stretching from it.

"Why?" he asked in his thundering voice. "Why are you not afraid? Do I not look like a monster to you?"

Glad that I had kept my hands over my ears to deafen the sound a little, I nodded. "Yeah, you do look like a monster. Doesn't mean you *are* one."

His claw froze in the air, inches away from my face. The sharp parts caught the dim lights from the city, reflecting them a little. It was oddly beautiful. His hand being so close to me also gave me a better look at his arm—it was covered in a glossy mix of feathers and thin hairs, and I found myself wishing there was more light so I could see it better. I almost wanted to reach out to touch them. They looked soft.

I leaned past the claw to grin at him. "If you want to scare me, you'd have to show me your angel shape. Now *that* would be terrifying."

"Lord Lucifer… showed you?"

I nodded. "Once. Actually, right after he showed me his Devil shape. I guess he didn't understand why I wasn't afraid, either."

I blinked, and Paimon was back to his human form, watching me with a slight frown on his face.

"You are an odd one," he said quietly when I finally took my hands from my ears. "What *are* you afraid of, if not a demon?"

"Water," I replied without hesitation.

"What?"

"Water," I repeated. "I'm scared of it. Well, not water, per se, but swimming, or being on the water. Big water, like the ocean, or a lake, or a river." I shuddered.

And Paimon laughed. He dropped to the ground, resting his arms on his knees as he leaned forward, doubling over in laughter.

"Did I say something funny?" I frowned at him.

He smirked up at me, taking a break from his fit. "You're so weird."

Somehow, this situation felt oddly reminiscent of when Lucifer had shown me his shapes. When he'd decided to stick around. He'd said the same thing, calling me weird and then making cocktails in my kitchen, making himself at home in my house.

I stretched out my hand to help Paimon up. "So, does that mean you have your answer?"

His face softened a little as he took my hand, turning into something much gentler, something that made my heart skip just one beat. "Perhaps."

Chapter 6

"Well?" Luce was bustling around my kitchen while I was trying to grab the few things I needed for work in a hurry. "How did it go?"

"Not now," I snapped. "I have to get to work!"

"Ames! Come on, just tell me: good or bad? Do you want to see him again?" Luce's expression was pulled into a pained grimace. He was far too eager to find out, and I was in no mood to go into the complexes of his underling before I'd even had tea. Especially since I was already running late. "I'll tell you tonight. Bye!"

Without heeding his shouts, I shut the front door behind me and rushed to my car. My phone rang, but I let it go to voicemail. As I folded into my car, I noticed how dark the day was—thick, grey clouds covered the sky and for just a moment, I looked back to my open bedroom window. I hoped it wasn't going to rain again today. Then again, if it did, I could just ask Luce to deal with it in exchange for a promise for sushi or cocktails. He would probably also appreciate me getting him some real coffee. Perhaps I should buy him some regardless.

I managed to get to work on time, but only because the streets were unusually quiet that morning. Kit was waiting for me at her desk, playing with a lock of her hair. No surprise there. Whoever thought it was a good idea to have a new person start on a Friday, anyway? She was guaranteed to have forgotten everything I'd told her last week. Hell, I'd have difficulty remembering in her shoes after two, almost three days.

"Morning, Kit!" I said, trying to force my way into cheerfulness. Maybe she wasn't as airheaded and pea-brained as I remembered her. Best to give her the benefit of the doubt.

She looked up at me and blinked twice, her brow furrowing a little in confusion.

"Good morning…" She trailed off. Then her eyes brightened. "Tanya!"

I made a face, my mood instantly dropping a few levels. "It's Amy."

"Oh, right! I'm so sorry." She smiled at me apologetically. "There were just so many new names and faces to remember, and I guess you kind of look like a Tanya."

Okay. I could understand being overwhelmed by meeting too many people at once. I supposed I should give her a pass for that one, though I really wanted to know in what way exactly I looked like a Tanya, and what exactly that was meant to mean anyway.

I came around the desk and took my seat, though a glance at her computer along the way showed me that she hadn't even turned it on yet. I pointed.

"Want to maybe… start your day?"

Kit, who had taken out her phone to furiously tap away at it, looked up at the screen dismissively. "Oh, I can't."

Her eyes went back to her phone.

"Um… Why not?" For good measure, I turned on my own machine, allowing it to go through its slow booting routine that lasted ten times longer than it really should have.

Kit shrugged. "I forgot my password."

"Oh, okay. Did you call IT?"

Mystified, she put down her phone and looked at me. "What for?"

I could tell, this was going to be another extremely long day. "To get you a new password so you can actually do your work?"

She shook her head. "I really don't see how a clown and some balloons could possibly help with that. Is this some kind of internal company thing I don't know about?" Her face brightened up. "Oh, is this like an initiation prank? Like in sororities?"

I couldn't do much more than stare at her. She looked back at me, unaffected and cheerful. Whatever was going on in that mind of hers, I didn't understand it. How did she jump from a forgotten password to clowns and then to sororities? It just…

what?

Unless… No way. There was no way anyone would mispronounce Stephen King's *It*. Right?

Clearing my throat, I decided to give up on understanding. It certainly wasn't going to help us start our day. "I think I'll just call Amanda and get her to help you, all right?"

Kit nodded enthusiastically. "That's a great idea — Amanda's so good with computers!"

I should hope so. She wasn't our IT person for nothing.

Picking up my desk phone, I dialed her number, but no one picked up. I supposed she was either running late or there was a fire to put out somewhere else. I sighed. There was really only one solution for the moment.

"Come here," I said, making space for Kit. "I'll walk you through the parts of the CRM we didn't get to on Friday."

Kit was almost instantly beside me. At least she was eager to learn. But as it turned out, I had to explain the CRM from scratch, as she had apparently forgotten all about it over the weekend.

After an exhausting morning, lunchtime wasn't much better.

Kit insisted on spending her lunch break with me, joining me in the booth in the staff kitchen, and began chattering on about her weekend. Truthfully, I only listened with half an ear. Usually, I liked to stay alone during lunch so I could take a break from concentrating. I didn't want to have to use my brain anymore, but talking with people meant thinking was a necessity. At least Kit didn't expect intelligent responses to her monologue.

"And then, we finished our drinks, and he asked if I was ready to go home yet, and I said *no*. So then he took me to this amazing club—it was so fancy, you wouldn't believe it. I don't even know how he got us in there, but he said that he knew one of the bouncers or something? Something about them playing football together. So anyway, we got there, and I was like, oh, em, gee, there are so many famous people here, right? And then we actually spoke to Carlos Mendoza, can you believe it? Carlos Mendoza!"

"Mhm," I said, chewing on my lunch. That name sounded familiar, and something in the back of my mind began ticking. Hadn't I seen him act in something recently? I couldn't quite put my finger on it, though.

"But all he wanted to do was dance with this other girl." Kit pouted, before brightening up again. "But she really was amazing, you know? That woman could *dance*! And there was this guy with her, amazingly good-looking and handsome, and they were like, on fire. Yeah! They really set the club on fire. I swear, *everyone* was watching them. And guess what happened then? She actually blew off Carlos

Mendoza. Can you believe it? Carlos Mendoza got shot down!"

She was barely taking enough of a break to breathe. I was honestly kind of impressed, but I was also a little concerned that she might soon be turning blue on me.

"I don't even know if she's famous or anything—but I guess she must've been if she was there. Rich, for sure. And I bet the guy with her was a model. You know…" She suddenly tilted her head to one side and gauged me. "You don't look that different to her." Then she gave a clear bright laugh and looked down at her food. "But she was way younger and less serious than you. She's the kind of person I'd love to be friends with, I'm sure."

Wait a minute.

That *had* been me. Kit was talking about me! She'd seen Luce and me dancing at the club, and the guy who'd tried to hit on me had been Carlos Mendoza! Before I said anything that might give me away, I stuffed some food in my mouth. Her words also made me wonder how old she thought I was. And what kind of person I was because her words indicated a pretty clear bias.

"Oh, by the way, I was wondering," she prattled on, luckily oblivious to my realization.

"Hm?" I offered, as though it mattered.

"My cousin David is in town this week, and I was wondering if you'd have time to show him around tonight? I wish I could do it, but I have a date and I *so* don't wanna cancel it!"

I stared at her. Either she thought I was a loner without any friends or plans, or in her mind we were already besties, meaning, she was either incredibly rude—or insane. I wasn't sure which option I preferred.

"Um." I was about to say *no* when her phone rang.

"Hey!" she answered it, her expression instantly brightening even more. "Oh, already? Sure, I'll come right down. Give me a second."

Jumping to her feet, she beamed at me and grabbed my wrist. "He's here! Come down with me so you can meet him!"

Even though Kit looked like a weak little snowflake, she had quite an iron grip. She pulled me after her, out of the office and down the stairs, dragging me right in front of a gorgeous man. Admittedly, I wasn't usually there for the white-guy-blond-hair-with-blue-eyes thing, but he made it work for me.

"David, this is…" Kit trailed off again, the same frown from this morning reappearing as she tried to introduce me.

"Amy," I reminded her.

"Amy," Kit repeated, turning her eyes back on her cousin. "She's been training me, and she's so helpful!"

David cleared his throat and stretched his hand

out to me. "It's nice to meet you, Amy. Thanks for looking out for my cuz. I know she can be a handful and a little absentminded."

"David!" Kit whacked him and pouted, but it didn't seem to faze him one bit. His dreamy smile was set on me, and the corners of my lips arched up before I even knew what was happening.

"Here are your keys, by the way," he said and handed them to Kit before winking at me. "Case and point—she forgot these this morning. I hope she's not causing you too much grief."

"She's no problem at all," I lied, "and I'm sure she'll find more people to look after her in no time." That part at least was true. I'd seen the looks some of our coworkers had been giving her, Amanda included when she'd briefly stopped by this morning to help with Kit's computer problems.

David's perfect lips quivered knowingly as he quickly glanced over at his cousin. "That is very kind of you to say."

Oh, he knew exactly what I wasn't telling him. And I had very quickly changed my mind about showing him around. I placed my hand on my hip and granted him my most charming smile. "Kit tells me that you're in town for a few days and need someone to show you around."

He chuckled softly. "Kit is well-informed."

"I'd be happy to offer my services, if you're interested."

Yeah, so I was flirting. No one could blame me, even if David was essentially a stranger and related to my least favorite person in the office. He was handsome. And I was single. There was nothing wrong with wanting to find out if our personalities matched as well as I could imagine our bodies doing.

His gaze flitted to his cousin with one raised eyebrow. Kit barely paid attention to our conversation. She was possibly too caught up with thinking about her own date to realize that she was setting us up on one of our own.

"How could I decline such a delightful invitation?" he said, the corners of his eyes crinkling gently.

"Then allow me to pick you up around seven. Are you staying with Kit?"

He nodded. "She's good enough to put me up for the time being. I look forward to it already."

I acknowledged the agreement with a nod of my own and turned to go back inside the office, to give them time to themselves, and to avoid getting flustered and saying something I might regret.

The second I had made it back to our booth to clean up my lunch, I exhaled, letting my entire body droop forward, half-lying on the table. I'd been so tense talking to David. It had been quite a while since a guy had this much of an effect on me just by looking good. Paimon certainly hadn't. Well, past the first few seconds at least.

Oops. I just remembered that I hadn't told Luce about my "date" last night yet. And now I was already going another with someone not related to Hell. Then again, surely, that wouldn't cause a problem, right? Since Paimon clearly had no interest in me beyond wanting to understand why Luce hung around, and Luce was all for me dating… there was no conflict of interest for the moment. Besides, it wasn't like Luce got to plan out my life for me. He already had control over what happened after; he'd just have to be settle for that.

I'd gotten Kit's address from her before I left work, headed home faster than I'd ever managed before—and potentially running a red light, but I wasn't sure—got ready for my sort-of-date, luckily without a run-in with Luce, and headed out again, driving to Kit's house to pick up David.

I spent most of the drive contemplating what I was going to do with him. Obviously, we would have dinner somewhere, but I was thinking about taking him to one of the evening street food vendors instead of a fancy restaurant. That way, I could give him a quick walking tour of downtown while we ate. I could take him past the most famous monuments and tell him a little about their history and meaning. Then I could perhaps take him to the waterfront, and we could enjoy the starlight… Scratch that last part. So close to the city, there was no way anyone was ever going to see any stars, a clear night or not. Besides, I didn't even know if I liked him yet—or he me for that matter.

Slow down, *chica. Calma.*

If I continued on with this overeager brain of mine, I was going to start planning a double wedding with Lynn before I'd even had a proper conversation with the guy. For someone who'd been indecisive about wanting to date, I sure was jumping in head-first now.

Arriving on Kit's street, I locked the car and walked up to the house that ought to be hers. It had a front yard and a porch and looked like it could easily house three or four bedrooms. How she could afford a place this nice at her age, I absolutely had no idea. My only conclusion was that her family was loaded, or that it had been a gift from some seriously wealthy benefactor. I wasn't going to lie; I was secretly hoping it was the former because that might just mean the same was true for her cousin. I mean what woman didn't sometimes dream of a gorgeous, charming, and wealthy partner?

David was the one opening the door, and as soon as he saw me, a bright smile flashed across his face, and he stepped out, closing the door behind him just a little too quickly. Before I could do so much as say hello, he had grabbed my wrist and pulled me down toward the road. Apparently, dragging me around was a family trait.

"Let's go, quick, before she notices I've gone," he said quietly but hurriedly. A little mischievous glint was sparkling in his eye when he looked back at me.

Bewildered, I didn't resist but quickly took the lead, guiding him to my car. Just as I drove off, the front door opened again and Kit emerged, still wearing the same clothes from work, hectically looking up and down the street. Once we'd rounded the corner, I glanced at David. "Care to explain why we had to make such a quick getaway?"

He sighed and grimaced at me. "She... can be a little overeager sometimes. In a way that could be interpreted as thoughtless and ignorant, I suppose."

My eyes on the road, I could only imagine his expression. His voice sounded like he truly regretted those features of Kit's personality. As if he felt responsible for them.

I shrugged. "I wouldn't really know—I've only known her for two days," I responded, though truthfully, I could definitely see where those ideas of his stemmed from. It didn't surprise me one bit.

"There's no malice in the things she does," David continued, now looking out the passenger-side window. "She just doesn't always think things through."

I nodded, unsure about how else to react. "So... what exactly happened?"

He sighed again. "She decided she wanted me to go out with her tonight and meet a woman she thinks I would like so we can double date."

A red light gave me the opportunity to glance over at him to see the miserable grimace he was making. I snorted.

"And so you thought your best escape route was with me?"

"Pretty much."

Oh, no, that grin of his was too bright. I couldn't handle it. Eyes back on the road, where they belonged. Just in time to see the lights turn green.

"Have you considered that this might also be a date set-up?"

"Not really. You're not the kind of woman Kit would try to set me up with," he said. What the hell was that supposed to mean? "But if it was someone like you, I don't think I'd mind so much."

Two fronts were starting to battle in my brain. One was the romantic side that was turning to mush with everything David said and just wanted to get on a white steed with him and ride off into the sunset to find my happily ever after. The other side, however, was the snarky, sarcastic side. It won. It always did.

"Ah, yes. Because you know me so well already, don't you?" I rolled my eyes.

He chuckled. "Fine, you called my bluff. But I guarantee you, Kit wasn't planning on setting us up. And that alone makes you a better candidate for company than her friend. She has... bad taste in people."

I had a feeling I didn't want to know what he meant. So I didn't ask. After all, there were plenty of other topics to consider. "So what brings you to town anyway? Work?"

"Yeah. I'm only here for a preliminary assessment. I need to check how bad the situation is, and depending on how big the job is, I might have to relocate here for a little longer."

Okay, was I being crazy or was this him basically telling me that he was likely going to be available for dating?

"What do you do?" I asked, trying to stay nonchalant.

"You could call me a sort of exterminator, I guess."

Oh. *Yuck.*

Just the thought of cockroaches and other little beasties made a shiver run down my spine. And he had to work with them—daily. Poor guy. On the other hand... It made me reassess my initial interest in him. While I wasn't exactly squeamish about bugs, I didn't want to date a guy if I thought that a cockroach might be hiding out in his sleeve, ready to jump out at me at any second. "And how is the assessment going?"

He hesitated to answer. "It's too early to tell," he eventually said. "I'm planning on observing the situation a little longer. Ask some questions, double-check the usual patterns."

He sounded grim, like he really wasn't looking forward to this part. I couldn't blame him. It certainly didn't sound pleasant to me. While it seemed weird to me that he would wait to deal with the pests, what did I know? I was no expert in the matter. "Do you like your job?" I asked.

"Do you?" He turned the question around on me.

I shrugged. "I'm good at what I do. There's something to be said for that."

He sighed. "Yeah. I suppose so. And someone has to do it."

He wasn't referring to *my* job. One look at his inward gaze, lost in the view outside told me all I needed to know for the moment. *Someone has to do it.*

Once we'd gotten out of the car, we mostly spoke about our surroundings. I told him about the town's history—all I knew about it from colonial times to now, which was probably a little more than the average person, but far from what a paid guided city tour would offer. I bought us hot dogs and then burgers to eat as we walked, and David listened to my prattle with interest, asking questions and making intelligent comments. Honestly, he turned the whole experience into a real pleasure. Eventually,

I'd said everything that I had planned on saying and more, and we'd ended up by the waterside. Like I'd foreseen, even though there wasn't a single cloud speckling the sky anymore, we couldn't see any stars. What we could see, however, were the city's lights reflected on the water, which was almost as good.

"Okay, now that you've told me all about town, how about you tell me something about you?" His clear blue eyes were set on me, as if intent on finding out about all my deepest secrets. Curious and warm, I couldn't resist.

I shrugged. "What do you want to know?"

"Let's start with your full name, shall we? That way, I can cyberstalk you later and find out your most embarrassing secrets from when you were thirteen."

"Hey!" I swatted at him, laughing, and he chuckled along.

"Okay, fine, I promise I'll only look at the good things that are written about you online."

"You will do no such thing!"

"Oh, so you *want* me to look at the embarrassments?"

He was teasing me. And I was loving it.

I snorted. "You're not getting anything out of me now. Too bad you spoiled your master plan with your over-eagerness."

"No fair," he pouted. "How about we trade, then? We each get to ask ten questions—any questions—

and then we both answer them."

I theatrically contemplated his offer and then equally dramatically reluctantly agreed. "I suppose that might be acceptable. You start."

He grinned. "What's your most embarrassing secret from when you were thirteen?"

"I can't believe I fell for that," I said, shaking my head. "Now you don't even need to type in a search anymore."

"Pay up, then. But don't worry. I'll tell you mine, too."

"What a relief," I said sarcastically, giving him a *look*. I gave the question a moment's thought before I answered. "I had a crush on my school's mascot. For like a month."

"I'm afraid to ask, but… what was the mascot?"

I cast down my eyes before looking up at him shyly. "A chipmunk."

"A chipmunk?" he echoed. "Seriously? A chipmunk?" He wiped a hand over his stunned expression. "I mean, I could understand a wolf, or a bear, but a chipmunk?"

I snorted. "You could understand a bear?"

He shrugged. "They're strong."

"And chipmunks are cuddly," I countered. "And you wanted embarrassing. I guarantee this is not something you could have found out with your internet sleuthing."

"I'll take your word for that." His body was

relaxed, making me feel at ease as well. This was so wonderfully *easy*. Nothing like my conversation with Paimon had been.

I leaned forward on the bench, resting my chin on my fist, and smirked up at David. "Your turn."

He sighed and turned his gaze up to the sky. "When I was thirteen, I choked on a piece of paper in the middle of a test."

"How did that happen?" I laughed.

He grimaced and shrugged. "I was cheating, but when the teacher came toward me, I shoved my cheat sheet in my mouth and tried to swallow it. That didn't go so well, though. You have no idea how hard it is to eat a whole A4 sheet of paper in one go!" He genuinely looked desperate to show me. "Needless to say, I got into a lot of trouble—once they determined I wasn't dying. I had detention for about a month."

We both laughed and turned our gazes back toward the waterfront.

"Your turn," he said.

Okay, time to find out if he was definitely single and I hadn't just been misunderstanding the signals. I was getting dangerously close to developing a real crush on him, and I didn't want this to go any further if he was already in a relationship. Especially since polygamy wasn't for me, no matter what Luce might think.

"What's your partner's nickname for you?" I

asked, hoping I was sly enough for him not to guess the purpose behind my question.

One of his eyebrows quirked up. "This feels like a trick question," he said. "I don't have a partner. But past nicknames include Bear, Goliath, Davy, Davy Jones, and babe."

"I don't think 'babe' really counts as a nickname, you know. But I see now why you said you could understand crushing on a bear mascot."

"Guilty as charged." He chuckled. "Then how about you?"

"Perry, Lia, Chiquitita, Milly, kitten, tiger, and…" I paused, a shadow of regret overcoming me for just a moment at the memory of Jonathan calling out to me. "Earhart. Also all past nicknames."

"Earhart?" David asked.

I nodded. "Amelia Earhart. I was named after her. Guess my parents hoped that I would take after her and become a pioneer for womankind." I shrugged lightheartedly, but a dark shadow fell over David's face.

"You're not sure why they named you that?"

"I never had the chance to ask. My mom decided on the name before I was born, and she died during labor. My dad found a new family, so we didn't spend a lot of time together. I actually grew up with my uncle, but he passed away a few years ago."

I could practically feel the jovial mood dropping. Way to go, Amy—making everyone uncomfortable with your past. Great job. A-plus.

"That must have been tough, growing up," David said quietly after a long, awkward break in which I was far too aware of my own breathing.

I laughed, hoping to break the tension.

"It really wasn't, surprisingly. My uncle was great, and I kind of considered him more my dad than my birthfather. I never felt like I was missing out by not living with him or spending much time with him. I would have liked to have gotten to know my mom, but at least I had her family. Aside from my uncle, they all still live in Ecuador, so I went to visit about once a year."

As David cleared his throat, his shoulders seemed to unclench a little. "I'm glad to hear that," he said. "Well, it's my turn again, I guess… So tell me, what's your biggest regret in life?"

His question elicited a chuckle from me.

"You went to the deep, dark questions real fast, didn't you? But let me think." Now, I expected that most people would have felt that selling their soul would be a thing to regret, and I couldn't pretend that it didn't cross my mind, but I didn't actually regret doing it, so much as I regretted the reason. I wished it hadn't been for Jonathan's sake, but for my own. Or at least someone who'd deserved it, like my uncle. But it wasn't really the kind of thing I could have mentioned in a casual first date sort of conversation, if ever. "My biggest regret is forgetting my best friend's birthday two years ago."

I grimaced at David as I recalled Lynn's disappointed, almost broken-hearted face when she'd realized. I'd like to think I'd made it up to her since then, but I still felt guilty every time I thought about it.

"Mine is—"

David was interrupted by my phone ringing out. Seriously, why was I getting so many calls at inopportune times recently? I checked the caller ID. Luce.

Silently, I cursed to myself. He only ever called me when I wasn't home and he felt he needed to talk to me quickly. Which also meant that if I didn't pick up, he'd show up in person in a few minutes, and I really wasn't ready for David and him to meet.

"I'm sorry." I grimaced, pointing at the phone. "I really have to take this."

"By all means." David's calm, understanding smile put me right at ease, and I got up and walked a few paces away before accepting Luce's call.

"What's up?"

"Where in the blazes are you?" he asked, though we both knew it was a rhetorical question. He knew exactly where I was. "I was close to sending out the hellhounds to sniff you out."

"You can keep them chained up." I sighed. "I'll be home soon."

While I would have liked to talk with David a lot

longer, taking out my phone had also made me realize the time. And I still had to go to work tomorrow. Unfortunately.

"You better. Need me to come get you?"

He sounded far too eager to teleport here for my liking.

"No, thanks," I was quick to assure him. "I've got my car. Why are you waiting for me, anyhow? Is something wrong?"

"Of course there is." The breath caught in my throat for a second. "I still don't know how your date with Paimon went. And you know I'm *dying* of curiosity."

I breathed out slowly, annoyed that he'd almost caught me. "Curiosity killed the cat," I muttered, but Luce was quick to counter.

"But satisfaction brought it back. Now get your ass home so we can drink while having this conversation."

He hung up. *Rude!*

But... knowing him, he would just come get me anyway if I wasn't at least on the way home soon. Sadly, I would have to cut this very pleasant evening short. *Curse you, Luce.*

"Hey..." I went back to the bench where David still sat, watching the water. "I'm afraid I'll have to head home. Mind if I take you back?"

He got to his feet. "Sure, that works. Thanks!"

He fell into step beside me, and we slowly walked

back toward my car, which was parked a few blocks away.

"So," he said casually along the way, "trouble with your roommate?"

I gave him a sidelong glance, but he was conveniently not looking at me. Instead, he seemed to find a lot of interest in the asphalt ground.

"A friend," I corrected. "I live alone. But I should probably start charging him rent, considering how often he's there."

"Must be a pretty good friend if you give him a key to use," David noted, a strange tint to his tone.

My brows twitched as I tried to place his expression. Was he mad? No, not quite. Troubled, certainly. Perhaps… jealous?

My heart beat faster at the notion. I'd now spent enough time with him to know that I would love to see him again, that I was kind of hoping something might develop between us. That he might be the one I'd take to Lynn's wedding as my date. But, sadly, he was only likely to be in town for a few days, and there was no guarantee that he'd come back, or that he liked me. Besides, he was related to Kit, and I wasn't sure I wanted more of her in my life. We weren't exactly the kind of people who matched well.

"I guess so," I said.

We barely spoke on the drive back to Kit's house, but when I stopped the car in front of it, David didn't get out. He looked straight ahead as I waited, almost as though he were fighting an internal battle with himself.

"Amy…" he eventually mumbled. "I… I, uh…"

I waited patiently for whatever he was trying to say, hoping that it was one thing, fearing it was another.

"I was wondering if I could see you again," he finally finished, turning his gaze up at me. My heart fluttered and my stomach did somersaults in response to his questioning look. My face growing hotter by the second, I nodded, smiling, because I didn't trust my words. I felt like I was a teenager again and had just been asked out by the hottest guy in school.

"Then… can we exchange numbers?" he asked.

Without hesitation, I handed him my phone as he gave me his and we punched in each other's digits. He took a little longer than I did, but I didn't mind waiting. With a somewhat troubled smile, he handed my phone back to me and opened the door.

"I look forward to next time," he said, and I could barely affirm my consent before he'd gone and opened the front door to Kit's place.

Even after the door closed again after him, I took a moment to breathe and to collect myself. Okay. This had turned into a date, and he wanted to see me again. And I wanted to see him again, too. This was… perfect.

Chapter 7

The smell of rotten eggs greeted me as I opened my front door, and I sighed inwardly. Truth be told, I wanted nothing more than go to sleep. It was just past midnight—already two hours past my usual bedtime for a weekday—and I felt wrecked. But, alas, Luce was waiting for me. And by the smell of it, he must have been jumping back and forth from Hell a lot over the past few minutes.

No sooner had I closed the door behind me than he skidded into the hallway from the kitchen.

"Finally," he cried. "I was about to just come to you."

"Thanks for not doing that." I sighed. "You would have made me crash, for sure."

He nodded earnestly. "Yeah, I figured you wouldn't like that. Turns out, it was a good thing, too, because look who showed up!"

A beaming and mischievous grin plastered on his face, he guided me into the kitchen, where I was met with another hottie from Hell.

"Hi, Paimon," I said levelly. "What are you doing here?"

"It's 'Cornelius' here," he corrected. "I don't want to raise any unnecessary suspicions."

Ah, yes, because turning into a hellish beast in a city park didn't count as raising suspicions, unnecessary or otherwise. Obviously. At least his presence explained the penetrant smell of Hell travel. He must have just gotten here.

"So what are you doing here?" I set my purse down on the counter. "Come to keep Luce company?"

A flash of displeasure crossed his expression when I'd mentioned Luce, but one eye flick to the Devil himself seemed to calm him down again. I glanced at Luce. He hung back, trying to blend into the background without missing any of the show. His gaze switched from Paimon to me and back again without interruption and he looked like he was on the edge of his seat. This conversation couldn't possibly be this exciting to him, could it? And yet, I could tell he was trying to soak up every word, gauge the situation, and affirm whether or not we had developed some form of romance. Apparently Paimon hadn't told him much more than I had then. Then again, it wasn't like there was much to tell in the first place.

You might be the Devil, but you are the worst match maker. Poor Luce. Well, Paimon was about to break the news to him, I was certain.

"Actually, I came to see you," Paimon said.

There were two sharp intakes of breath as Luce and I both simultaneously lost our composure.

"Wow, is that the time? Well, I've got some business, so toodles!" With a wave of his hand, Luce poofed—and he was gone with another swell of Hell stench. I wasn't going to be able to have any conversation while coughing my lungs out, so I raced to the kitchen windows and yanked them open, greedily sucking in the fresh air. When I trusted that the smell wasn't overwhelming anymore, I turned back to Paimon.

"Pai… Cornelius, correct me if I'm wrong, but I was under the impression that you'd found out what you wanted to know. Why did you want to see me again?"

I observed him, arrogance met with casual flair as he sat on the high stool, leaning against the counter, watching me in turn. The top three buttons of his deep-blue shirt were open, slightly exposing his chest. Almost casually, he ran his hand through his perfectly-styled black hair. Almost.

"As you have been continuously on my mind since our last encounter, I have come to the conclusion that you're worthy of receiving a little more of my presence. Besides, I'm still not sure I have uncovered all there is to uncover."

His dark eyes followed me as I walked around the kitchen after closing the window again. Taking a seat on the opposite side of the room, I could still feel their intensity on my skin, even when I wasn't looking at him.

"Um, I really don't think there's all that much more to me than what you've seen? I go to work, I chat with friends, I hang out with the Devil." I shrugged. "That's me in a nutshell."

Paimon's eyes narrowed as he contemplated me. "A likely story."

I felt like I was trying to convince a conspiracy theorist that his conviction was wrong. "You do realize I'm just a human, though, don't you? A 'mere mortal'?"

Paimon was practically glaring at me. Yeah, he wasn't buying it. It didn't matter that it was true, he didn't *want* to believe it. At this rate, I was never going to be able to go to sleep.

"What do you want from me?" I knew I sounded defeated—I certainly felt like it, too. Heck, if he asked me to go on another date, I'd say *yes*—against my better judgement—just to be able to go to bed already. My lids were starting to feel pretty heavy. I stifled a yawn.

"You will go on another *date* with me. And you will continue to do so, until I have figured it out."

Wait a second. Seriously? Had I just foreseen the future or what?

"Fine." I knew I was going to regret this later. I could feel it in my bones. The fact that I'd be going on a date with a demon while I was hoping for another date with a guy I actually liked… well, it didn't bode well. But my desire to get some well-deserved rest was stronger than my common sense. Call me the Chief of the Bad-Decision-Brigade if you liked. As long as I got to sleep, I didn't care. "But I'm going to bed now. I imagine you can let yourself out."

I left him in the kitchen and headed up the stairs. I didn't even care if he stayed in the house. Apparently, I just wasn't fazed by demons in my kitchen anymore. Fine by me.

A small draft of rotten eggs reached my nose when I reached the landing, informing me that either Paimon had left or Luce had returned.

A few minutes later, I was just pulling the covers over me when another draft hit my nose, and Luce barged in. I hadn't even gotten a chance to turn off the nightlight yet.

"So?" he asked excitedly, and far too loudly.

I decided to ignore him and cuddled down into my pillow, closing my eyes.

"Well? Are you guys dating? Do you have a second date planned? How did it go?" He climbed onto the bed beside me, leaning over me to make sure I was hearing him.

I punched out the nightlight, growling. "It went terribly, and yes, I guess I did agree to another date."

"Terribly? Why?"

Ugh. The universe was conspiring against me to

not let me sleep. Or perhaps it was just inconsiderate ex-angels who had no understanding about how important sleep could be to a human. Severely disgruntled, I turned to Luce, the shapes of his face illuminated half a foot away from mine by the slivers of streetlight that skittered through the open window and past the curtains.

"You have weird taste in friends," I told him seriously. "And please don't ever set me up with one of your fanboys ever again."

Confused, Luce furrowed his brows, but then a dawn of realization and understanding slowly crept into his eyes. He quirked up his lips in an apologetic grimace.

"Paimon can be a little… zealous, I suppose. What about Asmodeus, then? Or Beliel?"

I closed my eyes again, only giving him an incoherent grunt in response.

"Wait, no, you said you have another date. It might go better than you think, you know. I'll make sure to talk to him about human customs and how to treat mortals."

"Mhm. You do that."

I snuggled into the pillow, my mind growing groggier and more sluggish with every passing second.

"But if it doesn't go well, I'm setting you up with one of the others, you hear me? I think Bel would be a good call."

"Mhm," I agreed, only to get him to let me sleep.

I barely heard him say, "Sleep tight, Ames," and felt his hand pushing some of my hair out of my face before the land of dreams finally claimed me.

Tuesday basically didn't exist for me. I woke up late and groggy, somehow made it to work, and quickly passed the responsibility of Kit on to someone else so I could zone out without problems. I briefly wondered if I should ask her whether David had said anything about me to her but decided not to. First of all, I was basically a zombie who didn't have the energy to listen to her prattle on, and secondly it was just too high school. If he wanted to talk to me or see me again, he'd call or text eventually. Or I'd contact him when I was feeling more alive. Despite forcing myself to drink coffee, I didn't manage to wake up any more throughout the entire day. After work, I trudged home and dropped back into bed after having some small amount of microwavable food.

After a two-hour nap, I woke up again, my head fuzzy and a little confused, but after a few minutes and an ice-cold shower, I'd returned to being a mostly functioning human being. One glance at my phone told me that it was dead. Probably had been dead for the entire day, which would explain why it hadn't been ringing and buzzing and vibrating to interrupt everything I was doing.

I set it up to charge and slowly went downstairs to make myself some tea. As I waited for the water to boil, I looked through my calendar. I had nothing of note happening until Saturday for the Bridesmaid dress search. Well, unless Paimon was going to force another date on me in the meantime. Somehow, I got the impression that he wouldn't bother to wait until we could find some time suitable to me. He didn't seem like the type to bother taking a human's schedule into account.

Next week there'd be the cake testing, which reminded me that I needed to officially take the day off, or at least sign off for a half day. As far as I remembered, I had no meetings then, so it shouldn't create any problems.

All right. On to watch a bad movie before going back to sleep so I could be awake and functioning tomorrow.

I'd barely managed to put it on, when my phone rang upstairs. I really should have brought it down with me earlier. Rolling my eyes, I caved and trudged up to collect it. The letters *David* flashed at me from the lit screen, along with a new text message.

Hey, I was wondering if you're free tonight. I'd love to see you, and Kit mentioned that you seemed like you were having a rough day. Maybe I can help? David.

My heart warmed when I contemplated how sweet his intentions were, and how nice it was that he was hoping to cheer me up and wanted to see me. But I didn't even consider replying in the positive. I was wrecked and I both needed and wanted my rest. I didn't want to see anyone tonight, not even Lynn. So I quickly typed my reply.

Sweet of you to think of me! But I'm okay. I just need a little time to myself. Hope to see you again soon though!

I took my phone down with me, lest I should receive a message from Luce, threatening to show up if I didn't respond within a given time limit. It wasn't the first time he'd have done something of the sort, after all. Now that my phone had a charge again, I could see that I'd also had two missed calls, and a message from Lynn waiting for me. One of the calls was from my father, which I assumed I could safely ignore — he would contact me again if it was in any way important; he was probably just looking to borrow some money — and one was from an unknown number. I must have been added to another random spam list somewhere. Or it was Father Exodus trying to get my daily confession out of me. I had to assume he wanted to convert me to his cult or something. Anything else just didn't make any sense. Or he wasn't a priest at all, but some form of stalker who'd seen Luce and knew who he was. *Yeah, right!* I almost laughed at myself for the thought.

I checked Lynn's message, only to find it consisted of nothing more than a cat meme. Though honestly, that was exactly what I'd needed. It was cute, it was sort of funny, and it didn't require me to use my grey cells in the slightest. I sent back a laughing emoji, followed by a heart, and then finally started my movie. It was delightfully stupid and nonsensical, especially when it turned out that the monster mole not only lived inside a volcano but created them. That, and the ham-fisted acting was exactly what I'd needed to help me relax. I cuddled into my comforter on the couch and didn't resist when my eyes began to droop. I'd done worse things than fall asleep on the couch. I was an adult, so I could do whatever I liked anyway. And I was so glad I didn't have a dog that I might have still needed to take on a walk...

I woke up in bed the next morning, my phone blaring out my alarm next to me. My best guess was that Luce must have shown up at some point over the night after all and just carried me up. Or teleported me—who could say?

My suspicion was confirmed when I found a note on the kitchen isle in his handwriting.

Ames—sleeping is meant to happen in beds, not on couches. I can't always be there to look out for you.

He'd crudely drawn a cute devil face underneath

it.

I couldn't stop a smile from appearing on my lips. It was nice to know that he was concerned for my wellbeing. It was things like this that really showed me that he cared, that I wasn't just a random human he saw as a plaything or hobby.

I froze.

Why?

It was a question that I'd often posed myself back when he'd first stuck around, when he'd been there to bring me tea while I'd been crying about Jonathan, when he'd taken me out partying to take my mind off my ex, when we'd started watching bad movies together. Why?

He was the Devil—in charge of a whole otherworldly domain that I couldn't even fully fathom. So why squander his time here with me? We weren't romantically involved, he certainly didn't get close to everyone he made a deal with, and I was just another human woman. So why?

Paimon had asked the same question, and now it returned to the forefront of my mind as well.

How had Luce come to care for me? And why? Of course, I could argue that it must have been my enchanting personality and my good looks, but I just didn't believe that was all there was to it. I could be kind of a bitch sometimes, and I was fully aware that I was on the chubby side, which, by the way, I had absolutely no problem with, but I imagined that it kept me from being considered the most attractive woman in the eyes of society.

I could probably have squandered a few hours pondering this utterly useless question, but I snapped out of it relatively quickly. It was the way it was. Luce and I were friends and the reasons why he'd made that choice didn't really matter. Besides, I needed to get to work so I could ask for a day off next week.

Chapter 8

Work was uneventful. I got my stuff done, didn't have to babysit Kit anymore since she'd been given her first real tasks, which she managed to do relatively effectively, if a little slow, got Carol to sign off on my day off for Lynn's cake tasting, and was on my way back home before I knew it.

There was one thing I noticed as soon as I parked the car out front of my house: Something was wrong. I couldn't put a finger on it right away, but looking at the place, standing peacefully in the same place it always did, I could feel that something was off.

Before I even left my car, I looked up and down the street, but I could see nothing that seemed out of place there. Chiding myself that I was probably being paranoid for no reason, I grabbed my purse, and headed for the front door. Still, I felt uneasy as I inserted the key in the lock.

After only turning the key forty-five degrees to the right, the door swung open. Surprised, I stared at it. Had I forgotten to lock it this morning? I'd been deep in thought about Luce's reasons for being my friend; had that kept me from locking the door? It was possible. At least, I couldn't actually remember doing it. Even though I never forgot to lock my door, wasn't it said that there was a first time for everything? Maybe I'd been more tired than I'd realized.

Despite the fact that I was rationalizing my fear away, a queasy feeling in my stomach remained. I closed the door as quietly as possible, listening into the empty house for any unfamiliar sounds. Without so much as taking off my shoes or letting the keys out of my hand, I grabbed my phone and tiptoed through the ground floor, looking into the living room, peeking behind the couch—lest someone should be hiding there—and scoured the entire kitchen before finally gathering my courage and going upstairs, with a brief, uneasy glance at the door to the basement.

Now, here was the thing. I considered calling Lynn or Luce for backup. But I also reasoned that I didn't want to call either of them if there was nothing to worry about and I was just being paranoid. Luce, because I didn't want him to tease me about it, and Lynn because she'd have to travel quite a bit to get here. Especially since she probably wasn't even home from work yet herself.

I checked every room. Every single room. Even the attic. There was no one there. And yet the bad feeling intensified with every room I checked.

Finally, I just stood in the bedroom, after having

checked underneath the bed and behind the door and inside the wardrobe, of course, staring blankly at the carpet in front of me, trying to will my brain to put the pieces together and just tell me why it was so insistent that something was wrong. There had to be a reason, dammit!

When my phone suddenly buzzed, I dropped it and almost screamed with surprise. I caught myself and dropped to the floor as well, to make sure I hadn't cracked the screen. An unknown number was calling.

Don't pick it up, don't pick it up!

I picked up.

"Hello?" My voice was quieter and shakier than I would have liked, but at least it wasn't a whisper. Visions of men in black suits with guns and knives raced through my mind, along with threats and warnings.

"Hello, Amelia? Are you all right?"

A familiar voice. A concerned voice.

"Father Exodus!" I sighed in relief. I didn't think I'd ever been so happy to hear a priest. Or a con artist.

"Are you all right?" he repeated. "You sounded a little… off."

"Yeah, I'm okay. I was just a little rattled, that's all."

"I see. How come? Do you want to talk about it?"

The concern in his voice was so sweet, it made me

smile.

I giggled. "My overactive imagination just acted up a little, I think. It's all right though. By the way, you call me an awful lot. Don't you have people in your actual congregation you need to look after? I don't even know where your church *is*."

A moment of silence followed my words. Then he cleared his throat. "To tell you the truth, my order doesn't serve a single community as such. Our calling is that of a higher purpose, and as such, we go where we are needed."

I leaned against the frame of my bed, letting my legs sprawl out in front of me. "And you've decided that I need you? I should tell you that I'm not actually very religious."

Because knowing that the Big Guy existed kind of took the need out of believing. Knowing that my soul was going to go to Hell no matter what I did meant that there was no point in praying, either, never mind that Luce had practically told me that it did no good anyway because his dad didn't exactly care all that much about being worshipped. Well, at least not more than a celebrity did. Meaning he liked the attention but didn't really see a need to respond in any shape or form except on occasion. If he really felt like it.

"You don't need to be. I am here to see that your spiritual self can one day take the path to the Heavens, whenever your time has come. That is my prerogative, not yours. But, Amelia, are you safe?"

He was awfully insistent about finding out about my situation. And the frequency with which he called me was a little stalkery, too.

I lazily looked around myself. Nothing special here.

Everything was in its right place, the window was closed, the light was off…

I froze, and my gaze slowly returned to the window. It was closed. Shut properly, intentionally. Except that I always kept this window open. Luce never closed it, either, unless I asked him to, and I was certain that I had left this window open this morning when I'd left.

And now that one oddity had revealed itself, the other slightly out-of-place things I'd seen during my sweep suddenly became clear. The toilet seat cover had been up, even though I always put it down. The magnets on the fridge had moved ever-so-slightly, the clothes in my washing basket didn't have the newest stuff on top anymore, and one of the drawers in the kitchen hadn't been closed all the way, because it stuck sometimes just at the edge. Luce and I both knew the trick to closing it properly, but no one else would. Most people probably wouldn't even notice that it wasn't fully closed.

A million small inconsistencies, and yet they'd manifested in a weird feeling in my stomach. I'd known something was wrong. Someone had been here. Someone who shouldn't have been.

"Amelia?" Father Exodus's voice reached me from a million miles away, but it sounded muffled, faraway, and barely reached my consciousness.

Someone had gone into my home and gone through my things.

Heat followed by cold rushed through my body, turning my legs to jelly, and made my heart race.

What did they want? Would they come back? Had Father Exodus been involved? Was this why he was so focused on me?

I didn't know what to do. I didn't believe that they'd stolen anything. At least, I hadn't noticed anything missing on my preliminary search, and I didn't have that many valuable things to begin with. So what had they come for?

I bit my lip to stop it from quivering.

I needed to figure out my next step. First, call the police and a locksmith. Second, see if anything had been stolen after all. Or maybe do that first?

No, first, police and locksmith. I didn't want to accidentally wipe down any fingerprints, and I definitely didn't want to give whoever had been here a chance to come back tonight while I was probably failing to sleep.

"Amelia? Talk to me. What's wrong?"

I would give anything to have a friend with me right then. Not a stranger on the phone whom I was suddenly deathly afraid of — a friend.

As if he had heard my silent wish, Luce suddenly stood in the door, a mild smell of rotten eggs alongside him.

I looked up at him, bleary-eyed, still on the floor because my legs had turned to jelly, and he grasped at least part of the situation instantly when seeing my face.

"Luce," I whispered, my voice unable to give more volume. The tears came, and he dropped beside me, taking me into his arms without saying anything more. "Luce," I repeated, my whole body trembling.

No one had ever broken into my house before. And I'd never known the fear that came with that violation of a stranger infiltrating my safe spaces and rummaging through my stuff—including my laundry. Whoever had come here had tried to cover the majority of their tracks, but they hadn't been careful enough. But why? Everything on this day seemed to revolve around that small word.

Why?

I couldn't breathe. My lungs were trying to suck in air, but none would go in, my chest burning with pain. I was turning into a carp, grasping for oxygen, but my lungs burned, unable to receive anything.

Luce, identifying the problem without difficulty, grabbed my back-up inhaler from my bedside table and brought it to my mouth, helping me take a hit. And then another.

I calmed down and air returned to my lungs, filling them, soothing them.

Eventually, I had calmed down enough that I could allow Luce to help me stand up. I realized that my call to Father Exodus was still running, and I hung up without saying a word. I couldn't explain. I didn't want to justify myself to a third party who had nothing to do with any of this and couldn't help except by asking God to help me. Never mind that I suddenly felt convinced that he might have been involved in some form.

Luce and I went downstairs slowly, with him constantly keeping a close, concerned eye on me. He sat me down on a chair before making me some tea. I sat in silence, still trying to process my situation, debating whether or not there was any point in calling the police. What could they do? Nothing had been stolen as far as I was aware. And I didn't have concrete proof that anyone had been here. They could easily wave it away as hysteria, absentmindedness, and some Latina trying to make herself appear important. Even if they did believe me, they'd just tell me that I shouldn't have left the window open, that I'd had it coming to me, or something of the sort. Ask me if I was certain that I'd actually locked the front door.

"What happened?" Luce asked gently as he slipped into the seat beside me, placing a freshly brewed cup of tea on the table in front of me.

I gulped as I tried to sort my frenzied thoughts into some sort of order.

"Someone was here," I said, staring into the colored liquid. "While I was in work. They went through my stuff."

Luce rubbed my back with slow, gentle movements and I could feel the comfort and safety in his warmth. I leaned against him, uncertain where I should go from here. I just didn't feel safe. I felt violated, in a way, like my innermost secrets had been exposed and exploited. And I was terrified just thinking about the possibility of *them* coming back. I didn't want to abandon my home to leave it there for the taking, but I also didn't want to be here on my own.

"Luce," I pleaded, seeking his eyes with mine. "Will you stay here tonight?"

He didn't hesitate to nod and pull me into a tight hug. "Of course."

His skin was warm, as though the fires of Hell were coursing through his veins. After a few moments, I pulled away from him. There was still some stuff I had to do. First, call a locksmith. I took out my phone, but my fingers trembled too much to even dial the numbers. Before I could ask him for help, Luce pulled my phone from my fingers and dealt with the calls for me. Unfortunately, it seemed that no matter how many locksmiths he called in the area, they were all closed for the day or too busy to come by on short notice. Apparently, waiting for tomorrow was my only option. Guess I wasn't heading to work then. There was no chance I'd leave the house without having exchanged the locks first, so I took my phone from Luce again and shot a quick text to my boss, explaining the basic situation.

Hey, Carol, I can't come into work tomorrow. Had a break in. Call me if anything urgent comes up. Amy That should do. Carol was probably the best and most easygoing boss I'd ever worked for. I could rely on her not chewing my head off, and to not gossip to others about what had happened. I genuinely liked her a lot. Sometimes I thought that if I were a more social person, we should meet up for drinks and would probably get along pretty well.

I sighed and drank some of my tea. Even though I was still shaken, my head was clearing up and my confidence was returning to me. I gave Luce a crooked smile. "Thanks for being here."

"Ames," he reprimanded me mildly, carefully. "You know that whenever you need me, all you have to do is call my name. I'll be here."

"Yeah." I leaned across the kitchen isle, letting my cheek rest on the marble countertop. "Why, though?"

"Why?" Luce blinked, confused.

"Yeah. Why are you here for me? Why are you my friend?"

Luce chuckled in response. "Because I like you, dummy."

The doorbell rang.

I stared at Luce wide-eyed, fear that had only just begun to dissipate returning to my blood like dry ice. He took my hand and squeezed it, smiling at me with reassurance.

"I'm here," he said quietly, and I nodded, gaining strength from his presence.

The doorbell rang again and even though I flinched, I stood up.

"Wait here," I told Luce. I could do this on my own. I didn't need him to open the door for me or to hover over me to protect me. It would be fine. I could handle whoever was at the door. Real people I could handle. It was the unknown aspects that terrified me about my current situation.

Despite my mental reassurances, I walked toward the door impossibly slowly. By the time I'd reached it, the bell had rung out twice more. Latching the chain lock and my heart racing, I opened the door just a crack and peeked out to see who was there. "David?"

His hair was tousled, and his shirt was a little wrinkled, but my heart was bouncing between surprise and the joy of seeing him.

"What are you…? Hold up." I closed the door and removed the chain before opening the door again, properly this time. "What are you doing here?"

"I, uh…" He was frowning ever so slightly and looked down into the hallway behind me. "I was thinking about you."

His eyes returned to mine, and I thought I saw a tint of relief in them. He must have been concerned I wasn't there because it had taken me so long to answer the door. *How sweet!*

"Oh," I said awkwardly. I would have liked to invite him in, but Luce was there, and as much as I thought I might like David, flirting wasn't really on the forefront of my mind right then. "Thanks."

Least romantic answer ever. *Good job, Amy.*

"Um, I'm a little... occupied tonight, but would you like to have dinner tomorrow?" I asked, hoping to make up for my blunder.

David smiled his perfect smile and shook his head, his baby-blue eyes expressing immense sadness. "I can't. I need to leave tomorrow morning to report back to the headquarters of my organization."

"Oh." This timing couldn't get any worse, could it? Well, so much for another date with the charming handsome man. Guess I had to go back to dating Luce's Hell Kings. "I thought you were staying a whole week?"

David shook his head. "I was, but... I got the results of my assessment sooner than expected, and they're worse than I'd feared. But I will be back soon to take care of it, so maybe I can take you out then?"

Never mind the Hell Kings. I still had a shot with this dreamboat!

I nodded, feeling my ears heat up with excitement. "That'd be nice."

A smashing sound originating in the kitchen made me flinch, and it was quickly followed by the unmistakable smell of rotten eggs.

"What was that?" David asked, alarmed. His back and arms had tensed, and he took a step toward me, his gaze fixed on the end of the hallway, just before the kitchen.

"Nothing!" I shouted, trying to stay between him and the kitchen. "That was just my…" Cat? Dog? Goat? "Luce."

Dang it. He was too close to lie. Stupid Angel presence.

"Your Luce?" David's eyes darkened, and a brooding, looming presence seemed to take a hold of him. Somehow, the way he looked at me now inspired fear once again. Seeing him like this made me believe that he was capable of doing very bad things. And not of the sexy variety. My mouth was dry, but I could only stare at him. I could explain. I should explain. Say it was my friend with boundary issues. My roommate. *Anything!* But somehow, I couldn't force a single syllable to cross my tongue, and I just stared at David for an impossibly long time.

"I've got to go." He swished his back to me and walked out the door. Even though I was also relieved, I felt like I had just lost something. And while I wasn't exactly psychic, I knew for a fact that there was no way he would possibly ever call me again, job in the area or not. A man in my house that I clearly didn't want him to meet? I knew exactly what he was thinking. And yet, my thoughts were too scrambled to speak and clarify.

And yet, just before David left entirely, he turned to me once more, a gentle, pained look in his eyes, and he lifted his hand to my cheek, brushing it softly. "Take care of yourself, Amy. Don't do anything you might regret."

Still, my words were failing me, and I continued to stand in the doorway, looking out into the street even long after he'd driven off.

He'd just said farewell. And all because Luce had been here, as, I was beginning to suspect considering the stench or rotten eggs, might be one of his Hell friends and I was willing to make a bet on which one. I supposed, David's reaction wasn't surprising: A man in my house I didn't want him to meet, after I'd taken so long to answer the door in the first place, and didn't invite him in... What else was he supposed to think?

The kitchen door behind me erupted.

"Human—Amelia, I wish to speak with you."

Paimon. Yup, I'd called it. Feeling equally resentful and resigned, I closed the front door, and turned to him, glaring. "What?"

To his credit, Paimon seemed taken aback for just

a moment.

"I *said*, what?" I snapped at him. I pushed past him, and, startled as he was by my outburst, he didn't even resist when I shoved him out of my way. I walked straight into the kitchen, where I plopped down on a chair, continuing to glare at both Luce and Paimon, who had filed in awkwardly after me. Both of them watched me like schoolboys with guilty consciences.

I took a moment to take in the situation and somewhat collect myself. Then I pointed at the window.

"One of you had better open this window to get that smell out of here. Seriously, how can you stand Hell with all that sulfur stinking up the place? Secondly…" I gestured toward shattered porcelain on the floor, which appeared to have once been my favorite mug. "Whoever destroyed that, clean it up right now."

Paimon opened his mouth to say something, but I cut in before he had the chance. "*After* that, we *might* be able to have a conversation."

I was fuming. All my fear had been replaced with anger that someone had had the audacity to violate my home. Paimon and Luce ruining my chances with David had done the rest of it, and my broken mug was just the cherry on top.

Neither demon nor Devil argued. Within moments, the kitchen smelled and looked normal again and I sighed, letting go of some of my anger. "Now then…" I managed to give them a small smile. "What do you want, *Cornelius*?"

Paimon glanced at Luce before clearing his throat and letting go of his uncertain demeanor to return to his usual arrogant manners—shoulders squared, chin jutted forward and a cold look in his eyes. "I came to determine a suitable day for our date. Lord Lucifer was kind enough to inform me that schedules matter in the human world."

"Not interested," I said without a trace of emotion. I got up to grab myself a new mug from the cupboard and put the kettle on with warm water from the tap to speed up the process. After all of this, I needed another tea. Peach this time, I figured. I liked peach tea.

"Not… interested?" Paimon echoed. His pronunciation of the words almost made me believe that he had never heard them before.

I turned to him and nodded. "Correct. I'm not interested in another date with you."

"But you said—"

I interrupted him. "I know what I said. And I changed my mind."

The kettle done, I took a tea bag and filled up my cup. The smell was divine. A sweet, fruity scent that smelled exactly like it would taste. I could practically feel the succulent fruit flesh on my tongue. With the cup in hand, I turned back around to the two men in my kitchen, only to find myself with Paimon's demon face only inches away from mine. In this shape, he almost took up the entire room. His legs were still right next to Luce, at the other wall, but his hands reached across the kitchen isle, the long, spindly limbs keeping his body so high I was afraid he might burn himself on the ceiling lamp.

"You agreed to another date," he said, his voice as demonic as it had been in the park previously, as though a hundred voices in agony spoke in unison, while a grater worked away at shaving metal. And loud. My ears were ringing with every single word that came out of his mouth. The flaming balls that served as his eyes stared right into my soul. Even though they were so close to me, I felt no heat coming from them. His smell hadn't changed, either. It was still the same very pleasant aftershave scent I'd come to associate with him. "And you will keep your promise."

I looked straight back at him, unimpressed. "No, I will not," I said evenly, and I brought the tea to my lips to blow on it. "And I would appreciate if you didn't just show up inside my house anymore. It's troublesome."

I ducked underneath his arm and then underneath his leg past Luce to get to the door. Luce, wide-eyed and his lips slightly parted, seemed to be confused about the situation, but I'd have time enough to explain later. One person at a time.

"Oh, and by the way…" I turned back to Paimon to shoot him an icy glare. "Trying to intimidate someone into going out with you? Not classy."

I left him in the kitchen and let myself drop onto the couch in the living room. A few seconds later, I heard a screech like nails being dragged across a chalkboard, and like an angry centipede, Paimon scrambled after me, moving faster along the ceiling than I would have thought it possible for something of his size. Truth be told, it looked like a scene from a horror movie. He stopped inches away from my face once again, pinning me into my seat.

"You will regret that choice," he promised. "I will make you love me."

Uh. What?

"Paimon!"

Paimon jerked back from me, his fiery eyes flickering blue with fear, and he turned to look at Luce in the door frame. This was possibly the first time I'd ever seen Luce angry. Even though he still retained his human shape, blue flames danced along his entire body, and even his eyes had gained an otherworldly quality. His voice seemed to be more booming, as though it was amplified by all his Hellish power, but not painfully like Paimon's had been in the park. He glowered at Paimon, his nostrils flared, his entire posture exuding power. "I hereby order you to never enter this house without Amelia's permission again. She has given you her answer, her choice. Respect it."

Paimon snarled, a gesture more reminiscent of an animal than a human, and he poofed away, leaving behind only the usual stench. Almost as quickly, Luce's flames were gone and he was back to the same man I'd come to know, hurrying past me to open the windows.

I didn't say a word. I'd be lying if I claimed that Paimon's final outburst hadn't scared me a little. I hadn't expected him to be so... passionate. And so unable to take a rejection from a creature he considered below him. Well, okay, I could see how that might have been frustrating. I didn't even want to imagine how much lower I'd sunken in his opinion after Luce had put him in his place.

Clutching my warm, sweet-smelling teacup like a lifeboat, I squeezed my eyes shut. This evening was officially too much. I couldn't handle any more. If even one more thing happened, I would scream. And I meant loud enough that it could be heard on the opposite side of the planet. Even if Lynn called me now, it would have to go to voicemail. Maid of honor or not, I was not in a mental state where I could think about a wedding.

Luce sat down next to me. "Hey," he said quietly.

I opened my eyes to look at him. "Hey."

"Who was at the door earlier?"

I sighed. "A guy I liked."

"What? You didn't tell me about that! Who is he?"

Luce's surprise was only topped by his smile. It was nice that he could seem so pleased for me, even though I had just royally shut down his friend. Were they friends? I didn't really know. Paimon was his underling, certainly, but friends? I couldn't see how I would be able to tell. It hadn't really seemed like it.

I grimaced and shrugged. "I didn't really have a chance to. I only met him Monday. But I don't think I'll be getting a second date now."

The cold of the night was starting to creep in, and I shivered.

"Here." Luce grabbed a blanket and tucked me in. I didn't resist. "I'm sorry," he then said. He looked to the ground, and he genuinely seemed troubled, his brows tightly knit together, his mouth curved down. "I had no idea that Paimon would be… like that."

"It's okay. As long as you've got my back, I'm not worried."

The tension finally starting to leave my body, I was beginning to feel otherworldly levels of exhaustion, so I leaned against Luce. He put his arm around me, offering me his chest to lean against.

Chapter 9

The smell of freshly baked pancakes was a treat even my sleep-loving subconscious couldn't resist. I stretched languidly under my soft sheets, surprisingly feeling very well rested. We'd gone up together last night, and Luce had spent the entire night beside me upon my request, which was a good thing because even with him here, I'd jerked awake at several points, certain that I was hearing another intruder, but Luce had put me at ease, promising me that there was no one.

I'd been lucky to have him around, and I felt like I had never appreciated him more than I did now.

I swung my legs out of bed and trudged downstairs in my sweatpants and T-shirt, thankful I didn't need to go to work today. I was glad I'd texted Carol before Paimon or David had shown up, otherwise I would have definitely forgotten. She'd texted me back, telling me that I should look after myself and not worry. As I'd mentioned before — best boss ever.

When I reached the kitchen, I had to blink twice to accept what I saw was reality. Luce was flipping pancakes in the air before catching them again with the pan. He was also wearing one of the aprons I had stuffed in the back of my closet, a yellow one with frills and a pocket shaped like a pink cupcake that I was pretty sure had been a gift from my *abuela* in Ecuador.

"The Devil being domestic," I mused aloud. "My, if your Kings could see you now." I took a seat at the kitchen isle, grinning at him.

Luce smirked right back at me. "Then we'll just have to keep it a secret from them, won't we?"

He put a loaded plate in front of me and provided me with a choice of syrup or hazelnut spread. I decided to go with the syrup, drowning my pancakes in the tough, golden liquid.

"By the way," he said, "I called a locksmith again. She'll come by around two o'clock."

I glanced at the clock on the wall. It was already almost eleven. I really had been exhausted, huh?

"Thanks." I took a bite of my pancakes. Oh, delicious fluffiness, I just wanted to put all of it inside of me at once. Only after I'd finished off half my plate did I realize that Luce was watching me with furrowed brows.

"I'm okay," I promised, smiling. "If you need to go to take care of your own business, you should. I'll be fine."

Luce seemed hesitant and sighed. "I do need to go. At the very least to have a chat with Paimon."

I nodded, understanding, and he went on, suddenly avoiding my gaze. "And I hope it's okay, but I contacted Lynn. She said she'll come by around noon to see how you're doing."

I stopped mid-chew. Like always, he'd done far more for me than he'd needed to.

"Thank you, Luce. I mean it." I meant it from the bottom of my heart, but he only grimaced.

"At least half of what happened last night is kind of my fault anyway, so… I feel like I owe you."

Snorting, I returned to finishing off my meal.

"I'll be back tonight. Think you can handle yourself that long without me?"

Back to his teasing, joking ways already, huh? I grabbed a dish towel that had been lying on the isle and chucked it at him. "I'm perfectly fine without you, you know. I can handle myself." I chuckled.

His eyes twinkled. "Oh, I don't doubt that."

And he was gone. At least he'd had the foresight and good sense to open a window ahead of time, so the smell his disappearance created vanished before it ever got a chance to become intense. Alone for the first time since I'd realized the intrusion the previous day, I slowed down my eating. My ears quickly became more attuned to every single sound around me. It was quieter now, and it made every other sound seem so much louder. I finished up the meal and stuck the dirty dishes in the dishwasher before grabbing speakers, connecting them to my phone, and letting my favorite playlist bellow through the house while I took a shower. By the time I was refreshed and ready for the day, the doorbell rang.

I let Lynn inside, and she fell around my neck. "Amy, are you okay?! I'm so sorry I wasn't here for you!"

I laughed, shaking her off. "I'm fine, I promise. Luce was here and the locksmith is coming in two hours."

Lynn moved past me toward the kitchen. "Well, I'm going to be here with you the whole day. I got the day off work when I said it was a personal emergency, and I intend to use it to look after you."

"Look after me? You know I'm an adult who can look after herself, right?"

Lynn shrugged. "I guess. But you're also my best friend and I intend to show you how much I care about you, so get your ass over here, take a seat, and then we're going to be eating these chocolates, drink this black tea I bought, and do these crossword puzzles together."

One by one, she grabbed the corresponding items out of her bag to show me how serious she was. Crossword puzzles were her highest step on our friendship ladder. She meant business. She was going to make me spill the beans about everything, wasn't she?

Well, almost everything.

I didn't resist her kindness. Before long, we were

both lounging on the living room couches, plopping chocolates into our mouths in between gulps of tea, and everything was good with the world as far as I was concerned.

"Hm… Let's see…" Regarding the puzzle critically, I tried to determine which clues should be easier to get. We'd already covered about half. "Obscure, difficult to understand. Eight letters."

Lynn reflected on it for a moment, staring at the ceiling in concentration while plopping another chocolate into her mouth. "Esoteric?" she suggested, but a glance at the puzzle showed that wasn't going to work.

"Second letter is a '*B*.'"

"Hm." Her lips were moving as she contemplated other options.

I wasn't idle, either. My face crunched up, I pushed synonyms through my head at Formula-1 speeds. But only one came to mind that had a *B* in second place. Unfortunately, *Obscure* only had seven letters, not eight, and was already part of the clue.

"Abstruse!" Lynn shouted so loudly, I flinched.

That could work. I entered the letters and moved on to the next clue. "Sign, four letters."

"Symptom!" Lynn yelled and I threw her the crossword puzzle.

"Four letters, I said!" I yelled back. "It's gotta be *hint*!"

She glanced across the puzzle and wordlessly

added my suggestion. "Four letters—"

"Fish!" I interrupted. It was always fish. Well, sometimes.

Lynn rolled her eyes. "Would you maybe let me tell you the clue first?"

"Is it fish, though?" I grinned.

She didn't respond, instead showing me the back of her head. I celebrated my tiny victory as silently as I could manage, though some of my snickering probably still reached her ears. It almost definitely reached her ears. I wasn't being super quiet.

It only took a moment for Lynn to join me in laughing wholeheartedly and setting the crossword puzzle aside.

"Okay, now real talk, though." Sobering up, she swung her legs from the couch and turned to look at me. "You're still pretty pale. Are you doing okay? Are you eating right? Sleeping well? Taking breaks?"

I nodded dutifully to each of her questions, though I hesitated a little at the "taking breaks" part. "Well…" I mumbled. "I'm taking a break now?"

The last few days had been a little *hectic*, after all. Lynn's troubled frown told me that she was not happy with the response.

"Hey, Amy… If life is becoming too much right now, I can take the maid of honor duties off you, you know? It would at least be one thing less to worry about."

"No!" I almost shouted. Quickly, I collected

myself and lowered my voice. "No, please don't. I love helping you prepare for your big day. I *want* to do it. And if I'm being honest, if I don't help you as much as I can… I'd kinda feel like I'd have failed you as a friend."

"Oh, no!" She reached over to me and flung her arms around me. "You could never fail me! You're just perfect."

"No, *you're* perfect."

We both giggled.

"Guess we're both perfect goddesses. How about a drink to celebrate our divinity?"

"At this hour?" Lynn raised a perfectly shaped eyebrow. I was still stunned at how she wasn't a model. I knew she'd been approached when we'd been in college, but she'd never shown any interest in trying it out.

I shrugged. "Goddesses deserve worship and offerings, but we're fresh out of acolytes right now, so I figured wine was the next best thing."

"Bring it on then, I guess." She chuckled.

That was all the encouragement I needed.

We popped open a new bottle of one of my favorite wines—a surprisingly cheap red from a local vendor—and I poured it into my largest glasses with gusto. We clinked them together delicately before both taking rather large gulps.

"So then, how's the job going? Any exciting new clients?" I asked.

Lynn rolled her eyes. "You wouldn't believe the stunt Raymond was trying to pull the other day. But you know what, let's not get into that now. We've got a new intern, some kid from Richmond High. It's meant to be part of some new career testing scheme. She's with Bri for now, who, by the way, I've left in charge today." She took a sip from her glass. "We've got three big events to deal with right now, all happening within the next four weeks. It's a little stressful, but it's manageable. It still gives me more than enough time to manage my own big event." She laughed, a delightful sound that always brought a smile to my lips as well. It was infectious.

"Are you sure it's fine to take time off for me, then, if you're so busy?"

Lynn shrugged. "Of course. Brianna knows what she's doing. And as long as Raymond doesn't get any more insanely stupid ideas, we'll be golden. Besides, I've told both of them that any big-scale decisions still need to go by me, so they'll call if there's anything urgent."

I was still impressed that Lynn was a high-level executive of an event management company. It was a rather large company, too, with locations in cities all across the world, though each location only contained small offices of a few people who handled everything. Here, Lynn was the boss.

"It's so cool that my best friend is a kick-ass boss lady." I grinned, mentally comparing her job to my own.

Lynn grimaced. "I'm just glad they're not trying to do to me what they did to Melissa before."

"Wait, who's Melissa again?"

"She was my boss before. I think you met her once? But when she got married, they pushed her into a desk job because they thought she was going to get pregnant and abandon the field."

The field. It was what Lynn's people called the active jobs that required travel and constant calling back and forth to organize events.

"Did she?" I asked. "Get pregnant, I mean."

Lynn frowned at me, pursing her lips. "Yeah, but that's not the point, you know. A pregnant person can do this job just as easily as one who isn't, with the exception of a few weeks and maternity leave. And I guarantee you that the only reason they're not moving me is because I'm marrying Taylor."

"So," I tried to summarize, "you're annoyed that they don't treat women different to men anymore?"

"No!" Lynn slammed her glass on the table, glaring at me, and probably the world in general. "I'm annoyed because they're treating me differently than a straight woman!" She paused and then added, "And that they're treating any woman like that, or, I should say, person with a womb. They even did it to Tony, you know, and he's a trans man. He didn't even want kids! But they didn't care. It's like the only thing that matters to them is whether or not they might lose money because someone has the capacity of getting pregnant."

"And they're not worried about you because you're marrying Taylor."

Lynn nodded, her eyes sparking with anger. "I don't even want to know what they'll do when I *do* get pregnant."

I nodded sympathetically. She'd told me a while back that she and Taylor both planned to get pregnant, ideally from the same sperm donor, so they could both have blood-related kids who were related to one another as well. It was a nice idea, I thought. And I'd already enlisted my help with the raising years ago, since I didn't actually want kids of my own. Although I had the feeling my hypothetical kids would have loved playing with their Uncle Luce.

"Speaking of, I was wondering…" Lynn suddenly wasn't quite meeting my eyes anymore, and she was actually blushing. "Do you happen to know if… uh… Do you think Lucian might be willing to, you know, help us out?"

She gave me her biggest puppy-dog eyes, but I only felt horror. That was a terrible idea. And I should know, being the queen of those. I didn't even want to imagine what a Devil-angel-human spawn of his would look like. And I definitely didn't want a burden like that going on Lynn.

Sorry, Lynn. I'm going to lie my ass off to save you.

"I'm afraid that won't be possible," I said, making a face. "He doesn't like to talk about it but..." I pointed to my nether region. "He's not exactly *functioning*, if you know what I mean?"

Lynn's hands flew up to her cover her mouth.

"Oh, gosh, he's... Really? Oh, poor thing. I'm glad I didn't ask him directly then."

She looked both horrified and like she pitied his very existence. Not surprising, considering that she considered bearing children her ultimate success in life, and she now thought he might be impotent.

Sorry, Luce. But you'll have to play along on this one.

"Best don't bring it up," I advised her, hoping that I could keep this little white lie secret from him.

She nodded pensively. "How's *your* work going, by the way? Didn't you get a new recruit? Beat them nicely into shape yet?" She playfully punched the air twice.

I sighed, thinking of Kit. "She thinks I'm old and boring," I grumbled. "And I'm kind of wondering how she managed to be hired."

"Old?" Lynn gasped and broke into laughter. "I mean, boring, I'd understand, but old? You're thirty-one!"

I shrugged. "I know. But hold on a minute — what do you mean you'd understand boring? I'm not boring!" I huffed, already sorting what arguments I could use to prove that I was an interesting person. Sadly, the biggest points I could come up with were my friendship with Luce and my past dancing days.

Grinning, Lynn leaned back in her seat and took a sip of her wine, sarcasm oozing from every word. "No, of course you're not boring. You have so many hobbies, after all. And you read so many books, and you try out so many new things."

In a bout of childishness, I stuck my tongue out at her. "First of all, reading books is not necessarily a mark of an interesting person. Second of all, I do read books, thank you very much, and third of all, I'm very open to trying new things. I just don't often come across the chance is all."

"Uh-huh." Lynn smirked, and I gave it up.

So I wasn't the most exciting of people when you excluded Luce's presence in my life. So what? Maybe it was *because* of him that I didn't get to do all of those things interesting people did. He did take up a lot of my time, after all.

"So tell me about this new girl. What's so bad about her?" Lynn asked.

Grateful that we were moving the conversation away from my personality flaws, I embraced the not-so-smooth subject change and went on to tell Lynn everything that bothered me about Kit as a co-worker, starting with her inability to grasp simple concepts and her lack of motivation to do anything that she wasn't explicitly told to do. My rant went on to include the fact that she'd used me as an excuse to get rid of her cousin for a night but then decided to get David to ditch me without telling me because she'd had a different idea.

Lynn whistled. "Damn, girl. She sounds like a piece of work. And you actually ended up showing the guy around town?"

I nodded and blushed a little. "It was kind of a date. He's really cute. And charming." Then I remembered the previous night and the disaster with his sudden appearance on my doorstep and sighed. "But I won't be seeing him again. I kinda messed it up."

"What? How?"

"Well, he came by yesterday, and Luce was here helping me out after the" —I gestured in the air with one hand—"thing."

"And let me guess, he thought you guys were…?" I nodded and she groaned. "Did he give you a chance to explain at least?"

I hugged my wine glass close to my chest, as though it could provide any level of comfort. "Not really."

"And this right there is why I don't date men anymore."

"Huh?" I stared at her, baffled by whatever she might be trying to tell me.

"Misunderstandings," she clarified. "Men seem to always jump to conclusions and assume they're right no matter what. It means they won't talk things out, and it just overcomplicates everything."

"Down with the patriarchy," I mumbled.

Lynn watched my face for a moment before reaching out to the table and picking up another box of chocolates. "Need a substitute lover?"

I sighed with relief and gratefully took the chocolates from her. "Always."

The door rang and I looked at Lynn, bewildered, unable to imagine who might want to talk to me in the middle of the day on a weekday.

"You should probably open that," she noted, so I heeded her advice and answered the door.

The person on the other side was a rather short, stocky woman roughly my age with short, cropped, dark hair and a cheerful attitude, dressed in dungarees over a branded T-shirt that displayed her company's name and logo across the chest. Her cheerfulness was contagious. "Hi, I'm from Parson's Locksmiths. I was told you needed some help changing the lock of your front door? This is the Perez house, isn't it?"

"Yeah, you've got the right place. Thanks so much for coming!" I sincerely hoped I wasn't slurring my words yet. It was difficult to tell how much alcohol might affect my outer appearance, and simultaneously be altering my perspective of the situation, after all. "It's, uh, this door right here."

I pointed dumbly at my front door and her grin widened.

"I had a feeling that might be it. All right, it won't

take long. You can just relax. Where will you be when I'm done? And do you need me to do the back door as well?" She cocked her head, and I was struck by how cute and yet cool she looked. I'd never really considered dating a woman before, but if it was someone like her, then…

Whoooa, hold up, inebriated brain! What is happening?

Was I interested in women too and had never realized it before?

"Um… Mrs Perez?" She was waving her hand in front of my face and I caught a glance of a name stitched onto the T-shirt just under the company logo. Samantha.

Suddenly, I realized that I was staring at her. I shook my head to clear my brain. "Oh, uh, sorry! Yup, I'll be just over there," I pointed at the door to the living room. "Holler if you need anything, okay? And yes, if you could also do the back door, that'd be great! It's just… uh… back there. Um, also it's just 'Ms.' I'm not married."

I smiled stupidly, instantly questioning why I put so much emphasis on telling everyone I was unmarried.

"Alrighty then, I'll get to it. Be done in a flash," Samantha chirped, apparently unbothered by my strange behavior. She walked back to the street, presumably to grab some tools from her car. Meanwhile, I returned to the living room and let myself fall back into the couch beside Lynn, staring straight at the ceiling.

"I think," I said quietly, "I have my first girl crush."

Lynn stood to attention almost instantly. "You have your *what*? Are you sure?"

I looked at her, analyzing the typical signs of a crush in my head. Hot ears—check. Tongue-tied—check. Staring—check. Contemplating their looks—check. Wondering how they'd be as a partner—check. The only difference seemed to be that this one was a woman. A first for me. I nodded.

Two crushes in one week; I felt like I was back in high school.

"I gotta see this girl." Lynn jumped up to peek around the doorframe. A moment later, she returned to the couch, nodding her approval. "She's cute. You could ask her out, you know."

I considered it for a moment, I really did. But when I thought how that had ended the last time—yesterday—and how busy I was going to be over the next few weeks... It seemed more prudent not to. I didn't want to drag anyone into this mess right now. Besides, something told me that I hadn't seen the last of Paimon. He'd been... too angry. And he was too obsessed with Luce.

Most of this feeling was probably just due to the alcohol in my system anyway.

Plus, I knew that Luce hadn't given up on his dream of setting me up with another one of his Kings and I really didn't want to ambush anyone at their work and ask them out. That felt all kinds of icky.

I sighed. "Yeah."

The afternoon passed, Samantha left again, and eventually, so did Lynn. I felt safer again in my house knowing that the lock on the door had been changed, even before Luce came back.

And for the first time since I'd known him, Luce looked tired when he popped into my kitchen.

"You okay?" I asked, while stirring my pot of stew.

"Yeah." He plopped down on a chair. He even looked disheveled. Messy hair, his shirt not tucked into his jeans… Hell, I thought I could even see the hint of bags under his eyes.

"Sure?" I took out an extra bowl and set it down in front of him before I took the stew from the stove and poured it onto both of our bowls.

He grimaced. "Just… Paimon being difficult. I sorted it out, though."

I nodded, not wanting to pry. Luce had clearly had a tough enough day already. He needed a friend, not to recount everything. Besides, I wasn't sure I wanted to know what he meant when he said Paimon was being difficult.

"Movie?" I asked, and he'd never looked more relieved.

Chapter 10

Once again, I found myself in front of the bridal shop, this time in my own car with Luce in the passenger seat since I wasn't planning on drinking like last time. I could already see Brianna and Hailey waiting inside, along with another two women I didn't recognize, probably Taylor's other bridesmaids. It seemed like the brides-to-be weren't here yet.

I slowly let out my breath to relax my shoulders. "Let's hope we can get this over with quickly," I mumbled, and we got out of the car.

Upon entering the store, the heads of all the women snapped over to stare at Luce. It was like someone had suddenly turned on the lights. Well, at least it meant they weren't looking at me. That state lasted for all of two seconds. Two of the women, Hailey and a white woman with chestnut shoulder-length curls, moved their gazes to me and yup, what had just been admiring and flirtatious looks turned into hard, icy glares instantly. What was it with these women and their catty attitudes?

I walked over, ignoring the glares, and took a seat

near Brianna, who was greeting me with a smile instead.

"Hey," I said quietly.

"Hey," she answered equally softly. "I heard you had a break-in this week. You okay?"

Of course. With Brianna working with Lynn, I'd kind of forgotten that she would probably know about what had happened. I nodded. "All good now."

I'd even closed the bedroom window before leaving. If I'd learned anything from this incident, it was to not leave anything open when I left. Something I was pretty sure my uncle had tried to teach me as a kid. A lesson that had clearly been lost on me until now.

Brianna's eyes flicked to Luce, who had immersed himself in an animated conversation with the other women.

Like moths to a flame.

I shuddered when recalling of the kind of flames Luce could conjure. The kind of flames that would burn these women if they got too close. The kind of flames even someone like Paimon respected and feared.

"Lynn mentioned your guy there had the perfect idea for our dresses."

"He's not *my guy*," I said. "But yeah, he has a hand for fashion. I'm surprised he hasn't started looking around yet, if I'm honest."

Just then, Lynn and Taylor appeared in the door, strolling hand in hand.

"Morning, everyone," Lynn called out cheerfully. Taylor's hazel eyes fell on Luce, a strange expression crossing over them. Lynn gave her hand a quick squeeze, which didn't escape my notice. They crossed over to the rest of us and even the shop's owner appeared as if by magic. Or perhaps she'd been there all along, just blending in with the décor of the store. Luce detached himself from his admirers to meet them and Lynn cocked her head to one side.

"Have you had a chance to take a look around yet, Lucian?"

Instead of responding, he granted her a wide grin and whisked past her, walking goal-orientated to one specific niche in the store, and took out two dresses without so much as glancing either left or right. I had no idea when he'd found the time to spot them, so I assumed he had some kind of super-heightened awareness thanks to his... I wasn't sure what to call it. Species? Were angels a species?

Luce held up the two dresses so everyone could take a full look at them.

They were both variants reminiscent of a toga wrapping, in a silvery, sparkly grey. One of them had a few more glass-stone decorations along the waist, while the other had a stronger pastel-blueish tone to it.

Lynn and Taylor inspected them, looked at each

other, and smiled, before Taylor turned back to everyone.

"Lucian here had the perfect idea for the bridesmaid dresses, so we decided to let him pick them out for us. These are his choices, so we'd like everyone to try them on."

A few seconds later, the store's owner brought out a rack with the two dresses in various sizes on it. As all the women gravitated toward her, she handled them quickly and effectively, passing a dress to each of them depending on whether they were one of Taylor's or Lynn's bridesmaids. While I waited for the hubbub to die down, Lynn grabbed my hand and pulled me to the side.

"You doing okay?" she asked, peering at my face.

"Yup." I nodded and took her by the shoulders to turn her around. "But today isn't about me, you know. This is about you two. So go on, grab your champagne, and prepare to judge us all." I winked at her and gently pushed her toward the couch where Taylor had just taken a seat.

"Oh, wait, before I forget…" Lynn looked back at me over her shoulder. "Lucian apparently found the perfect dress for Taylor, so they'll just be checking it for size tomorrow. Taylor's already got a picture of it and she said that if it fits, it's the one."

"That's great!" I'd been cut out of the loop, seemingly. Then again, if Taylor loved the dress, wasn't it a good thing? Still, it felt like I'd been dishonorably discharged from service. It was my best friend's wedding and I wanted to help her as much as I could, after all.

Good thing I was doing something right now to distract myself. I let Lynn take her seat and joined the queue of women to grab the dress I'd be wearing to my best friend's wedding—it was one of the ones with glass gems.

I slipped it on in the changing room and it felt like the dress had been made for me. The material was silky-smooth, flowing along my skin like a gentle brook. I was the last one out, and even though I could see how great the others looked in their dresses, the breath caught in my throat when I glimpsed myself in the mirror.

The dress hugged my figure in the most flattering way possible while hiding the body parts I wasn't comfortable showing. Looking at my reflection, I couldn't help but feel that I looked like a Greek goddess. It was beautiful. But I wasn't in any danger of upstaging Lynn. Or Taylor, if I trusted Luce's judgement, which I did.

Taylor and Lynn clasped each other's hands, squeezing tightly, lips quivering, and before long, they both had tears in their eyes.

Then Lynn nodded, heavily, to the shop's owner. "They're perfect."

"Then we'll just do the stitching to get the measurements."

We all bought our own dresses, not wanting to put any more financial strain on the brides than they already had to carry. Besides, with dresses this pretty, none of us would have ever dreamed of complaining.

While some of the others were getting their stitching done, I looked at myself in the mirror again, admiring the dress and myself in it. So I was a bit vain. Big deal!

However, as I was swirling from side to side to see how the fabric moved, I caught a glimpse of something dark with two bright-red dots in the reflection behind me. My heart instantly beat faster, and I swished around to get a look behind me, outside where I'd thought I'd seen the shadow. But nothing was there. Just the parking lot, more or less deserted with the exception of a few cars. I could have sworn I saw…

But I must have been mistaken. I put my hand to my forehead, enjoying the pleasantly cool sensation. Maybe it was good Luce had taken over my job of helping with Taylor's dress. I must have been more stressed than I'd realized if I'd started to see things that weren't there.

One of the seamstresses trudged toward me, pins already between her lips, ready to be used. Except that she took one look at the dress and raised her eyebrows, surprised, before spitting out the pins into her hand.

"I don't think I need to do anything with you, dear. Looks like the dress was made perfectly for you."

She moved on to Brianna, and I looked at myself in the mirror once more. She was right.

For the first time in what felt like an eternity I could sleep in on Sunday.

And it was a proper sleep in, the kind where I actually woke up around dawn but then stayed in bed until past noon anyway, just dozing and snuggling into the comfortable, cocooned warmth I'd accumulated throughout the night. My favorite kind.

When I finally deigned to leave my wonderfully cozy nest, I trudged downstairs and made myself tea, both surprised and pleased that the house was silent. This might have been the first time in months that Luce hadn't here by the time I'd gotten up on a Sunday. It was nice to have a few moments to myself, to enjoy the silence.

It got boring real fast.

By the time I'd finished my first cup of tea, I was beginning to feel restless, wondering what I should do with myself. Maybe Lynn was right, and I really was a boring person. Well, I'd show her!

Determined to be neither bored nor boring, I got dressed, grabbed my purse with my phone, wallet, inhaler, and keys, and headed out.

I wasn't exactly sure where I was going, but I ended up by the waterfront, near enough where I'd been sitting with David not even a week ago. I still wanted to kick myself for how that had ended. Then again… Maybe it wasn't too late to call him, or at least message him.

I sat down on the bench and started composing.

Hey David, about the other day, it's not like you think! Let me explain.

I read over the words again, grimaced, and deleted all of them. The most clichéd approach to turn the situation around was definitely not going to work. That much I'd learned from movies and experience. So instead, I tried to begin anew.

I hope you got home okay.

Yeah, a much better start. It didn't sound guilty because there was nothing to be guilty about, and it made it sound like I genuinely believed he might respond. I continued.

Let me know when you're back in town. There are still some places I would love to show you.

Flirtatious, but not too out there. And it put the next move on him. If he never texted me back, that would be it. My mind made up, I sent it off.

Well, that was about all I could do. If he wanted to know what had taken place that day, he'd just have to ask. After all, it wasn't a crime for me to have a guy friend at my house, especially when I was feeling vulnerable. No one could blame me for that, and I didn't owe him an explanation, excuse, or apology.

Nevertheless, I felt a slight tug at my heart, wishing David would respond and go out with me again.

Almost as soon as I had that thought, I wanted to slap myself for it. He was just another guy, and no guy was worth pining after. If Jonathan had taught me anything, it was that. You'd really think I'd know better by now. So what if I never saw David again? It wasn't like I knew him especially well or thought he was the guy I was going to marry or some nonsense of that sort. He was a crush, nothing more, nothing less.

I looked out across the water, the stiff breeze finding its way into my clothing, cooling me down. The water was active, too, waves piling up and crashing down, creating little lines of seafoam on the surface. I wasn't alone there. Other people were strolling up and down the waterfront, some with their dogs, some cyclists, joggers, and parents with their kids.

Even though it was a nice day—windy, yes, but warm and sunny otherwise—a chill suddenly ran down my spine and I felt the urge to check my surroundings. There was nothing out of the ordinary, and yet I felt as though I were being watched. Experience had taught me to heed the feeling when my limbs turned restless and ready to run and I wasn't going to question it now—not after there'd been a break-in at my house and I'd had creepy visions of demonic, obsessed creatures stalking me. I headed home rather quickly. Perhaps a little quicker than I ordinarily should have, considering speed limits and traffic lights, but hey, I was nervous.

Just as I got to my front door, however, I found a bouquet of flowers sitting on the doormat. Confused and surprised, I picked them up and looked for a card, but there was nothing attached to it. It was just a random bouquet. I looked up and down the street in case whoever had left it here was still around, but not seeing anyone, I went inside, locked the door and put the flowers into a vase.

My mind ran through guesses as to who they might have been from, covering everyone from Lynn and Luce, to Paimon and David, and even briefly considered the possibility that they might have been from someone from work. I was really hoping that it was David and that the flowers were a sign that he felt bad about leaving so abruptly the other night.

I stared at the flowers for a moment, admiring the light blue, almost-lilac hydrangeas, mixed in with the white, star-shaped stephanotis, some gardenias, and even some tweedias. It was an odd mix, but it reminded me of a wedding bouquet. Struck by that idea, I took a picture of it and sent it to Lynn. Maybe this would help inspire her.

I looked at it for another moment until I realized I

was getting bored again. In my own home, I felt safe again, and the feeling of being watched had completely dissipated. It was still early afternoon, so I had to find something to pass the time. My gaze fell on the oven. I hadn't baked in quite a while.

I wasn't a good cook by any stretch of the imagination, but when it came to baking, I knew my way around the kitchen.

Before I realized what I was doing, I'd put on some peppy music, poured myself a glass of gin and tonic, and had taken out everything I needed to make muffins and Victoria sponge cake. The music went deep into my bones, and I danced wildly around the kitchen while I put the ingredients together, singing along whenever I knew the words—and whenever I didn't—and sneaking tastes of the batter whenever I could catch my breath for long enough. My boredom was gone in an instant and I was fully set in the moment, only disturbed once by a reply from Lynn on my phone.

So pretty!! New MoH duty: Help us find flowers.

I smirked to myself. Finding the right flowers to go with her dress would be a lot of fun.

Once I'd put all the batter into pans and muffin cases and shoved them in the oven before setting a timer, I got to researching, finding flowers whose colors would complement Lynn's dress without standing out or fading into the background too much. While I was at it, I received a text from Luce, showing me Taylor in a wedding dress.

To my surprise, it was the snowflake ice-princess dress that Lynn had tried on at her fitting, and it suited Taylor perfectly, even more so than it had Lynn.

I looked back up to my flowers on the table and had the perfect idea.

What if you get flowers that match Taylor's dress, and she gets ones that match yours? ¯_(ツ)_/¯

Lynn's response was almost instant.

YES <3

I smiled to myself, happy I'd been able to resolve something so quickly. This bouquet I'd received was perfect. The colors matched up with the pastel blue from Taylor's dress, and the white flowers gave it the wedding look. There was no doubt in my mind I could put together an equally lovely and festive bouquet with Lynn's colors for Taylor.

But first, baked goods.

The sweet, warm smell was permeating through the air, making me feel cozy and getting my mouth to water. Hoping that they'd be just as delicious and fluffy as they smelled, I couldn't wait to bite into one of those muffins. Opening the oven, I stuck a wooden chopstick into one of them and retracted it again. By the looks of it, it was still a little wet inside. The base for the Victoria sponge cake, however, appeared to be just right.

Humming along to the music, I took it out,

leaving the muffins in a little longer. I left it to cool for a moment, while I rummaged through my cupboard to find the right kind of jam. I settled on strawberry. While it wasn't traditional, it would still taste amazing. I also grabbed some cream from the fridge and started whipping it until it had the fluffy texture I wanted.

Before cutting the cake in half, I took out the muffins from the oven, leaving the tray on the stovetop so they could cool down out of the way.

Once I'd applied the jam and cream generously between the two halves of the cake, I took out some powdered sugar and sprinkled it on top.

The delicious smell in my kitchen made me want to eat it all immediately, to devour all of it in one go and not leave a crumb behind, but I tamed my urge and only took one muffin to taste test.

It was heavenly. The warm batter was still ever-so-slightly moist without being runny, and the chocolate chips had melted perfectly inside. There was nothing better than a freshly baked muffin. Except for a cup of Earl Grey along with it. Needless to say, I made sure to procure myself one quickly.

Satisfied with myself, I took the tea and the remains of my muffin, along with the bowls in which I had made the batter, into the backyard, enjoying the late afternoon sun while cleaning out the bowls with my finger and watching some small birds flitting around between bushes. It was moments like this that felt like complete bliss. Even though there was no romantic love in my life, I had wonderful friends who always had my best interest at heart and who appreciated me, I had a job I was good at, and I had my own home where I could enjoy peace and quiet. What more could I ask for?

Well, I supposed I'd like to know who left me flowers.

Was it really David? Or perhaps it was Luce, trying to show me the perfect bouquet to go with Taylor's dress, already thinking ahead to make my life easier. As if I'd summoned him with those thoughts, he appeared in the backyard in front of me. The light breeze took away the eggy smell instantly. He grinned at me for a second before frowning and sniffing the air. Then his whole expression lit up again.

"Did you bake?"

His eyes were almost sparkling.

I smirked at him and nodded, heading inside to grab the Victoria sponge cake and make him some coffee. Last time I'd gone shopping, I'd bought him some slightly better stuff, and a small French press, so I was actually able to give him real coffee instead of instant.

"This smells delicious." He sighed and helped me carry out two slices of cake while I carried his coffee and my tea.

"Let's hope it tastes that way, too," I said.

"Nice flowers, by the way."

So they hadn't come from him.

"Yeah, I thought a bouquet like that would be perfect for Lynn, don't you? It matches Taylor's dress."

"True! Are you going to put one together that looks like Lynn's dress, too?"

"Yup. I'm already working out what flowers should go in."

We sat down and he narrowed his eyes at me. "If you're dealing with the brides' flowers, can I do the bridesmaids' ones?"

I shrugged. "I don't care. Check with the brides."

He didn't need to be asked twice. He flicked out his phone and started typing immediately. Why in the world he was so interested in being involved in this wedding, I had no idea. But it seemed to make him happy, and he was doing an excellent job, so what was the harm? Besides, his help meant that I had more time off, and that I had someone to bounce my ideas off, so it certainly made my life easier.

He took a first bite of his cake and rolled his eyes in pleasure.

"I've missed this." He sighed. "You need to bake more often, you know. And share your gift with the world. It's such a shame to let it go to waste."

I raised an amused eyebrow. "My 'gift,' huh?"

He nodded while shoving more cake into his mouth. "You should think about opening up a bakery, or a patisserie, or, I don't know, a baked-goods store. Something that sells cakes and cupcakes and all this delicious wickedness."

"It's wicked, all right." I snickered, thinking of how much sugar I'd put into my baking today. Oh, well, gotta enjoy life to the fullest, right?

Truth be told, I'd always enjoyed baking. It was something that had connected me to my uncle, who'd worked as a pastry chef. We'd always baked together and there certainly had been a time when I'd considered following his example. But then life had happened, and I'd gotten into a job that paid better.

Besides, chocolate chip muffins weren't exactly difficult to get right.

I glanced back inside. There was still a lot of cake left over. And I felt like now was a good time to start thinking about my bridesmaid duties more actively.

"Are you planning to stay for a while?" I asked Luce.

He pointed at the cake on his plate. "As long as there's cake, I'm going nowhere."

Alrighty. Seemed like we were in the perfect position then. So I took out my phone and called Brianna. She picked up almost immediately. "Brianna Miller here."

"Hi, Brianna, it's Amy."

"Oh, hi." She sounded surprised more than anything else, if a little wary.

"I was wondering if you're free this afternoon?"

As event planners, I knew that both she and Lynn often worked weekends, but I hoped that she wasn't on call today, at least. I was in luck.

"Yeah, I'm free. Why?"

I almost sighed in relief. "Can you come by my place? I figured we could plan the bachelorette party. Luce is already here, and I'd like to get your input as well."

I could almost hear the smile in her voice. "Oh! No problem. I'll head over in a sec. What's your address again?"

I gave her a quick rundown of the best way to reach my street before hanging up. Okay. Three brains were better than one, and getting Brianna involved in this part was sure to make us more likely to get along. I didn't want her to dislike me. I was just bad with people sometimes. Especially women. I seemed to have a knack for saying the wrong thing at the wrong time. Or not saying anything when they thought I should. People were difficult. But hey—I was trying!

Chapter 11

The time until Wednesday flew by like a rocket ship: Brianna, Luce, and I figured out what we wanted to do for Lynn's bachelorette party and what date suited all of us best, I brought muffins into work and distributed them among my colleagues, I figured out the flower arrangement, and ordered the bouquets for the wedding from the florist—with Lynn's permission, of course. Occasionally, I got the odd feeling like someone was watching me, but I figured that it was just the stress getting to me, an after-effect of the break-in. I didn't hear from David, and I didn't see a trace of Paimon, either, but I did find flowers on my doorstep again both days after I got home from work, different color arrangements than before, pretty, but not helpful for my task regarding the wedding bouquets. Kit had begun to ignore me, even though we sat near each other, so I assumed that David had told her about the misunderstanding, and she now took it out on me. But it was finally Wednesday, which meant a day off work and filled with cakes.

Just as I was heading out the door, however, I got

a call from an unknown number.

"Hello, Father," I answered it cheerfully.

I was met with a moment of silence. Then, Father Exodus' bemused voice. "How did you know it was me?"

"Because these days, the only unknown calls I get are either you or some scam salesperson, and I decided to take a shot." I shrugged, even though I knew he couldn't see me.

"I see." He laughed quietly. "I wanted to check in on you."

"That's sweet, but don't you worry — everything is right as rain with me. But how about you? Everything going well with the Big Guy?"

"I thought you weren't religious," he countered, cheekily, and I smirked.

"I'm not. I don't pray to him, but I'm not denying his existence, you know." Quietly, more to myself than him, I added, "It's not like he could do anything for me anyway."

I looked at myself in the mirror in the hallway. I was all set to go: had my shoes, wore my jacket, had my purse on my arm and my keys in hand. Yet I felt reluctant to cut the conversation short. A part of me still suspected he'd had a hand in the break-in, especially since he hadn't called since that day.

"Amelia..." Father Exodus said quietly, almost pleading, but he didn't go on. He sounded guilty and a flush of disappointment and anger surged through my body.

Before I could say or do something that might create problems, or give away what I thought, I hung up. I had stuff to do.

As I got into my car, I threw back a look at my house, glancing at my bedroom window to reassure myself it was closed.

It didn't take me long to get to the venue for the cake tasting.

"Hey, girl," Lynn called just as I got out of the car. "Ready to eat till we drop?"

"You betcha!"

Within a few minutes, we were seated at a round table in a comfortable booth in the otherwise empty patisserie, and the store's owner, probably the most muscular Asian-American man I had ever seen, brought out a serving tray covered in small, bite-sized treats. Upon our request, he'd also brewed the black tea I'd brought as a palate cleanser.

As we admired how petite and elegant the cakes looked — all of them including some form of icing or miniature decorations — he started explaining what all of them were.

"Here we have a lemon-meringue mix, and this one is a plain marble cake with chocolate glazing. Over here you have a strawberry shortcake, tiramisu, banana bread, and carrot cake. On this side, you'll find caramel shortcake, black forest gateau, mint chocolate chip, and cheesecake with mandarin slices."

I picked up one that was made to look like a small, yellow flower and cut it in half.

"This one was the lemon meringue, you said?"

He nodded.

There was indeed a layer of merengue that melted almost as soon as it entered my mouth, and the sweetness of the sugars combined quickly with the sour taste of the lemon. Unfortunately, the sourness was still almost overwhelming, and I had to use every ounce of self-control I had not to start squinting and pursing my lips. I glanced over at Lynn, who seemed to have a similar reaction to the cake. Both of us quickly reached for our teacups to wash away the flavor. We were lucky that the store's owner had already made sure to cool our tea ahead of time or the taste testing would have been cut short on account of burnt tongues.

"I have to take care of the shop, but please use this to write down your thoughts. If you need anything, just ring the bell."

He handed each of us a pencil and a small sheet of paper with all the names for the different cakes and space below them for evaluations and comments and set down a dainty little bell on the table. As he walked away, I immediately crossed out the lemon atrocity. While some people might have liked this kind of cake, it wasn't the right thing for a wedding, where you wanted a dessert that everyone could enjoy. And above all else, the brides needed to like it, and a single look to Lynn told me that she, at least, didn't.

As we tasted our way through the small cakes and took notes, Lynn decided that it was the perfect time to ask about my nonexistent love life. "So, did you hear from David?"

I shook my head and shrugged. "I sent him a text on Sunday, but I never got a response, and his cousin is ignoring me, so I think that's over."

"Hm." She watched me curiously, as I took a bite full of carrot cake. Pretty good. It was nothing out of the ordinary, but almost everyone liked carrot cake. It was a good, neutral option. And I was loving the cute bunny icing stickers they'd placed on top. Totally unfitting for a wedding, but who cared?

"What about that Samantha? She was cute."

I looked up at her, bewildered. "Who?"

"The locksmith, from the other day, remember?"

Vague recollections of a seemingly spunky, short, black-haired woman returned from the depths of my memories along with what might have been a mild crush, or possibly just a little too much alcohol. "Oh, her. Um. No? You do realize this isn't some romantic comedy, right?"

"But she was cute," Lynn insisted, pursing her lips. "And I think she was flirting with you."

"I sincerely doubt that. She was just doing her job, and I guarantee you, I'm not going to harass her while she's working. Besides, I think it's good I'm on my own. Relationships are troublesome." With gusto, I stuck a forkful of strawberry shortcake into my mouth and lightly stabbed my tongue in the process.

"You know I'm not letting you come to my wedding without a date," she threatened, and I threw my hands up.

"Why? It's not like I'd have time for them anyway. I'm there for you, remember? As your maid of honor? Why in the world would I need a date?"

"So you can be the first to join us on the dance floor," Lynn pouted.

"Ugh, fine. Tell you what: I'll dance with Luce. He'll be there anyway, and I know he won't step on my feet. Sound fair?"

Lynn sighed dramatically. "I suppose you two look good dancing together. I guess he'll just have to break a lot of hearts that day."

"What about me?" I protested.

"Yes, yes, you too." She winked at me, and we both laughed. She took a forkful of one of the other cakes before asking, "and remind me why you and Lucian aren't dating? You guys are close enough, and it's obvious he cares a great deal for you."

I shrugged. "I've just never really considered it as an option. And I'm pretty sure the same is true for him. Which, by the way, we've discussed before? Like last year on my birthday?"

"I know, but I still don't understand why."

Because I know he's the literal Devil and he owns my soul.

"I guess maybe we just feel that we're not compatible or something."

"It's a pity." She sighed. "But it's his loss."

I chuckled, thinking about how I highly doubted that Luce had ever entertained the notion any more than I had. He was my friend—reliable and a little kooky at times. And also a former angel. He had his flings, but he'd never given me the impression that he felt anything more serious for a person than a brief, passing infatuation.

"Oh my god, this one is so good!" Instead of only taking a forkful of the mint chocolate chip muffin, Lynn was eating her half right out of her hand. I'd stayed away from that one so far because I personally didn't like my baked goods looking green, and I'd never been that big a fan of mint to begin with unless it was tea.

"I need this at my wedding." She closed her eyes in bliss, making a little happy sound.

"You have weird tastes," I said dryly. "And don't forget that part of that needs to make it home to Taylor so she can taste it too."

Lynn frowned at me. "But it's so good! She'll trust me to pick the perfect treat. And you."

I blinked at her, unimpressed. "You don't want her to taste it because you think she might say *no,* don't you?"

She guiltily brought her teacup up to her lips, studiously avoiding my gaze. "No?"

Her halfhearted response made me chuckle, and I shook my head. "Pack it into the tasting box and we'll choose two more for her to choose from, yeah?"

"Deal!"

I spent the rest of the day after cake tasting organizing everything for Lynn's bachelorette party, even coordinating with Hailey to make sure we weren't going to be taking both brides to the same venues.

Thursday and Friday I had to work late to catch up on leftover work from my day off because Kit still couldn't handle all of the workload she was meant to do on her own—an awkward interaction, to say the least, since now I had to help someone with her work while she was working hard to acknowledge my presence only just enough that I couldn't complain about being ignored—so it was already dark by the time I got out of the office to start my weekend.

I'd been the last to leave, and the empty parking lot reflected that. My car stood out as a lonely shadow in the underlit lot, right beside some bushes and trees that were part of a decorative initiative to make the business park look more appealing.

As I stood beside the vehicle, I scoured through my bag to find my keys but couldn't get a hold of them. I must've left them on my desk. I sometimes put them down there when I arrived, so I supposed I might have forgotten to pick them up again. I turned to head back to the office, the key card hanging at my belt, but a large, looming dark figure in my way made me freeze, two fiery-red flames burning their way into my mind.

"Did you like my flowers?" The thunderous sound made me instinctively cover my ears. Paimon.

I frowned at him, though he was no more than a wafting shadow in front of me. "That was you?"

All those beautiful bouquets left on my doorstep, sent by a guy who'd been actively told that he shouldn't approach me. Great.

"I understand that is a mandatory aspect of human courtship. Though I fail to understand why. Their beauty is so fleeting, their lives so short... Much like yours."

A long, spindly arm reached out and briefly held a lock of my hair. I didn't react.

"What do you want, Paimon?" I was creeped out, but I felt more annoyed and angry than afraid. Boundaries had been set, and he'd actively ignored them. It wouldn't be a stretch to assume that all those times I'd felt like I'd been watched by someone could be attributed to him as well.

He stepped closer. "I have been agonizing over

that question. And I have come to the conclusion that the answer is… you."

I froze, my face nothing more than a deadpan expression. "What?"

"I need to have you," he repeated patiently. "To own you. You have to be mine. I want you to be mine and mine alone."

I couldn't believe my ears. The words, some of which might have come straight out of a badly-written teen romance movie, sounded only threatening coming from a Demon King.

"Um… I hate to repeat myself, but… *what*?"

The flames of his eyes stared at me, bore into me. "Be mine." The unspoken words of *or else* lingered just at the edge of my hearing.

My heart was racing, and my entire body felt cold. The air was charged with tension and every fiber of my body screamed at me to run away, to get away from this monster. He didn't feel like he had before. Something flickered behind those flames of his, something… crazed, untamed. Something that made him very dangerous indeed.

And yet I couldn't give in.

"No." I spoke this one word with absolute confidence because it was something he needed to hear. He needed to accept my choice, intimidation or not. I would not budge. Besides, I *really* didn't want to date a stalker. Never mind that whole "owning me" thing was archaic and not something I would ever accept lying down. Also — *creepy much?*

"No…" Paimon let my response roll over his tongue as though he were trying to taste its meaning, to digest its content. His flames seemed to grow duller for a moment. Then another voice made both of us whip our heads around.

"She belongs to me," Luce said, striding out of the darkness, glaring at Paimon. "Her soul is forfeit to me, the Ruler of Hell. You can never have her. Besides, she said *no,* several times. You've never been the brightest, but you really can't take a hint, can you? Go home, Paimon. Get some work done."

"I need her." Paimon hissed, his flames brightening again, almost flaring out of their sockets. "And I *will* have her." He moved so fast I couldn't even see him. "I just have to take your place."

He lunged at Luce with bared fangs, but Luce blocked his attack with something that looked like a shield of light materializing around his right arm. In his left, a sword appeared, made from constantly wafting and shifting shadows. I couldn't look away as they fought, though their movements were too quick for me to follow. I had no idea who was winning. But I knew I was worried for Luce. My heart was aching thinking of him getting hurt.

Paimon attacked relentlessly, snapping at Luce with his fangs while throwing his claws into the mix. When Luce blocked and evaded the attacks, Paimon opted for speed and agility, practically teleporting behind Luce. But Luce could match his speed. He whisked around, blocking the last attack with his sword and cutting into Paimon's shoulder, which glowed with residual light after Luce retracted the blade. Only now that Luce had created some distance between them could I see that Luce hadn't come out of this unscathed, either. There were some grazes of fangs and claws along his arms, though I had never seen the attacks happen.

"Stop!" I shouted, when I was finally able to gather my courage. Neither of them reacted.

Okay. Time to go nuclear.

I steeled myself, praying to whoever was listening that this wouldn't get me killed, and lunged at the two of them. Luce backed off in time, but Paimon lashed out, almost like a rabid dog, and his teeth sunk into my shoulder, too close to my neck for comfort.

"Amy!" Luce shouted, terrified—a note I'd never heard in his voice before. How odd. Never thought of the Devil as someone who would fear something.

Pain surged through my body from Paimon's bite, making it hard to think of anything else. It was like burning poison was injected into my bloodstream. All of my body pulsed with heat and agony. But he wasn't done. He lifted me up by the shoulder with his teeth, dislocating it and sending a searing, sharp pain through the socket, and yanked me aside, like a dog might throw away a toy. I crashed against a tree, the impact knocking the air out of me, and slid down its trunk. My vision was going fuzzy and darker, but I could still hear Luce's angered cry before more flashing lights streaked across my vision. I was in so much pain, it was screaming at me from across my entire body. My lungs burned with every breath. Darkness was creeping in on me, and the back of my head was pulsing with my rapid heartbeat. I felt cold, though my skin seemed hot enough to spontaneously combust.

Please be safe, Luce.

I felt a warm touch on my cheek. My unfocused eyes regained clarity for just long enough to see David peering into my face with great concern. Weird. Why was he here?

"It'll be okay," he promised.

I barely retained my consciousness as David carried me away. He was going to get me to a doctor. He was going to look after me. There was nothing either of us could do for Luce. Besides, Luce should be fine, right? He'd be okay! He was the Devil after all, an angel. Despite my own predicament, I couldn't stop thinking about Luce. How strong was Paimon in comparison to him?

"Luce..." I whispered, hoping that, perhaps, David could help him somehow.

But David did not reply. Set down in the passenger seat of his car, I watched the city's lights fly by us so quickly, I felt like I was in a dream. And, despite the pain, or perhaps because of it, I was lulled into sleep.

Chapter 12

What was that scent? Mint? No, something more sterile, more dulled…

I opened my eyes to find a painted ceiling fresco of a grinning, chubby-cheeked baby boy cherub grinning down at me. I frowned back at him, dismayed.

Why? Just – why?

Deciding that the cherub wasn't going to answer my vague question, I slowly turned my head to take in my surroundings. The small room had little more than a bed and a miniature bedside-table altar in it, incense and marked candles burning atop acting as the only light sources in the room. A silver cross and a golden-framed glass goblet with a reddish liquid completed the altar.

Even though my body screamed at me with flashes of pain, I sat up. I was wearing some form of simple gown, like an elongated T-shirt. Underneath it, my torso was practically mummified in bandages, as was my head, I noticed upon closer inspection. My shoulder hurt like it was on fire. Regardless which way I did or didn't move, it was aching, throbbing, and stinging. So I decided, if it was going to hurt anyway, I might as well let it hurt while I figured out where I was because I knew what hospitals looked like, and this wasn't it.

There were no windows set into the rockface walls, only the one door. I inched my way over to it and tried the knob, but it wouldn't budge. I briefly considered throwing my weight against it to see whether or not I could bust it open, but somehow, considering my state, that didn't seem like the wisest idea. Besides, unless I'd been dreaming, I thought I vaguely remembered seeing David.

Which meant that he must have brought me here. If this was his house, as weird as it may have been, I didn't want the first thing I did to be wrecking his door. So instead, I took another look around the room in hopes of finding my stuff—my clothes as well as my purse, ideally with my phone inside. I didn't exactly know whom I wanted to call—Luce, Lynn, or David—but it was the only thing I could think of doing. To my dismay, my things were nowhere to be found.

I licked my split lip. I was parched. The chalice on the altar was beginning to look very inviting, even though I really didn't want to drink that ominous red liquid—whether it be wine, grape juice, or something else entirely.

I started banging on the door.

"Hello?" I shouted. "Anyone there? David? I'd like some sunlight, please. And water."

No response.

My body still aching with every slow move I made, I figured exhausting myself would do no good and lay back down on the bed. As I glared up at the cherub, his smile seemed to get more conniving and false with every moment. I was quickly learning to despise it.

I wondered if I could summon Luce by thinking about him. But instead, thinking of him brought back the memories of last night.

Paimon had turned on Luce. He'd attacked him. Over me.

I shot up, ignoring the pain, my heart racing. Paimon and Luce had still been fighting when David had spirited me away, which brought up three more issues. First: Was Luce okay? Had he won the fight? Did he have to kill Paimon? Second: How much had David seen? How much did he understand? Third: Why had David been there in the first place? Had he hoped to see me or had Kit forgotten something at the office and asked him to go in her stead?

My head was abuzz with frantic, somewhat panicked thoughts. I had no idea how to check up on Luce in my current predicament to see if anything was amiss, and I had even less of a clue how to explain the situation to David should he ask.

I lay there motionless for quite a while, only staring up at the ceiling, until, finally, I heard steps approach, just before something scratched at the door, and it swung open.

"Amy, you're awake," David said, smiling as he entered the room, looking the same way he always did.

"I sure am," I confirmed warily. I was sure he had questions, but then, as I'd established, so did I. First of all — why in the world had he locked me in here?

"Are you feeling okay?" he asked, looking me over. I nodded slowly, though I was watching him just as closely. He was wearing normal clothes, and there was nothing out of the ordinary about him. "In that case, come with me. There's someone I need to introduce you to."

He held out his hand to me, but I ignored it, instead moving past him through the door. It opened into a stone corridor with large, arched windows at the side. The architecture looked Gothic to me, but it wasn't like I knew a lot about that kind of thing. It could have easily belonged to some other building style. Plus, for it to be genuine, we'd have to be on a different continent. The reddish stone was well worn, as if hundreds of feet had walked on it for centuries.

The hallway was long and straight to either side, with plenty of doors leading to rooms, nay, cells, that I suspected looked a lot like mine had. Stepping up to the window, I caught sight of a courtyard where a lot of people wearing heavy, brown robes seemed to be hurrying to and fro, some carrying books, others gardening. There were a lot of them, and most of them looked younger than I would have expected. Most looked my age, in fact. Monks and nuns, huh? Well, that explained the altar and the cherub at the very least. I was in some kind of monastery that mimicked the European ones. Or some kind of movie set. But why?

"This way," David said, and I followed him. I was still walking on bare feet, but the stone was so smooth, I didn't mind, even though it was quite cold. I had so many questions about this situation, but the right words wouldn't slot together in my mind.

David led me down a winding staircase at the end of the hallway and out into the courtyard. As we crossed it, I saw the heads of every monk and nun turning and following us, staring at me in particular while narrowing their eyes or even clicking their tongues in a manner that seemed threatening to me considering my current position. In order not to be left behind with these scary monks, I made sure to step closer to David, keeping him within arm's reach. We entered a small chapel at the side of the courtyard. Any sound from outside, be it the singing birds or whispering of the trees in the wind, disappeared completely when the heavy wooden door shut behind us. The sound of it closing echoed through the chapel. It looked exactly like one would expect: rows of wooden benches, a large cross behind an altar up ahead, many frescos of saints, and colored windows designed to depict holy scenes as well. One unusual thing I noticed was that every fresco and statue and window, depicted either the Virgin Mary, or a demon or the Devil being slain by a saint.

"Mother Leviticus, we're here," David called out, his voice sounding hollow in the large space. But that wasn't all that was bothering me about it. There was something in his voice that reminded me of someone, and it was nagging at the edge of my brain. I was so close to putting my finger on it, but I just wasn't quite there yet. It was the way the voice echoed around the room that distorted it.

A hooded figure that had been hunched over to kneel before the altar rose from the ground and solemnly turned to us.

"Welcome," she said, in a booming, but not unkind voice, opening her arms wide as if to do her words justice. Her head bore a shock of red locks, her eyes a sharp blue. Despite her age, or perhaps because of it, she made a striking figure, the deep lines in her face and silver streaks in her hair only adding to her imposing stature. She was even wearing a full suit underneath her robe. Like she was ready to head down to the stock market just as soon as she finished her prayers.

"I would like to introduce Amelia Perez to you," David said, and he put his hands on my shoulders from behind. I froze, the nagging feeling in my head quickly turning to certainty. The name he used was not what he'd called me on our date. I was absolutely certain that he had never, ever called me that before. And yet, the way he pronounced it sounded so familiar. Like I'd heard him use it often.

Amelia.

Suddenly, I realized why his voice had sounded so familiar the first time we'd met. Why he'd shown up on my doorstep the day my house had been broken into. Why it'd been so easy to talk to him, like we'd already known each other. And I cursed myself for not having realized it until then.

"Father Exodus?" I asked, more incredulous than concerned, and turned my annoyed gaze on him. He'd been playing me. And looking at what kind of place he'd brought me and what kind of situation he'd taken me from, I was starting to get an idea as to the why. My expression grew hard as I stared at him, seeking confirmation. He glanced at me and at least had the decency to blush a little.

"It's a pleasure to meet you, Amelia," Mother Leviticus said, striding toward us before David had a chance to justify himself, her heels clicking on the stone floor with every step. "There's a lot we have to discuss. I am aware of your predicament, and we're here to help you."

"Help me?" I asked, confused. "With what?"

I briefly considered if she meant Lynn's wedding, but there was no way. Some kind of religious order combined with David's reaction to Luce—well, I'd learned how to connect dots in pre-school. Best play dumb about Paimon and my pact with Luce. With any luck, they didn't know all that much about them or my situation. I was certain that I couldn't trust these people, not the least because David had clearly been taking advantage of me and had actively lied to me about his identity. Exterminator, my ass. Unless…

"Come with me," Mother Leviticus said. "Let us speak in my office. It'll be more comfortable there, and we can have some tea while we chat."

I'd never thought before that monks or nuns were all that keen on comfort, but I obeyed nonetheless, following her out into the courtyard once more and into a side galley of the main building. David was walking close behind me. Mother Leviticus walked a little faster than I could manage, my body still aching with every breath, never mind step, but I bit my lip and persevered as much as I could. Still, I couldn't match her stride. Before long, David stepped in, holding me up to take some of my weight. I glared at him, but I allowed him to help me nevertheless. I wasn't exactly in a position where I could pick and choose.

We quickly reached Mother Leviticus's office and filed in. To call it luxurious would have been exaggeration, but she certainly lacked the belief in the same kind of minimalist lifestyle I had been led to expect from devout worshippers by movies and

TV shows. The chairs all had a certain amount of padding, and there was an elegant crystal decanter of a clear liquid—I sincerely hoped it was water—sitting on the desk, along with several crystal glasses and a small plate of pralines. There was even a laptop on her desk.

We'd barely sat down, when the door opened again and a monk entered, carrying a tray on which sat a dainty tea set with a floral design. As soon as he'd placed it on the table, he left again, leaving me to wonder when Mother Leviticus had even had the time to ask for that tea to be prepared.

She now took the tea and poured us each a cup. I grabbed mine with trembling hands, slightly worried that I'd make the hot liquid slosh over the sides and burn my fingers.

"Let me begin anew," Mother Leviticus said, her smile almost as false as that of the cherub on my ceiling. "Welcome to the Ordo Sancti Matrem Suam. Recently, you've been contacted by one of our finest, isn't that right?"

She tilted her head ever so slightly to prompt me to a response. I glanced at David.

"Father Exodus," I mumbled, darkly. He looked away, as though he were ashamed. *Good. You should be.*

"That's right," Mother Leviticus continued, unperturbed. "See, we want to help you. And there's something you can do to help us, as well."

I narrowed my eyes. There was nothing about this situation that didn't make me suspicious, and I had a very bad feeling.

I tried to stand up, even though I was feeling weak and hurting. "I should go home. There are a lot of things I need to take care of."

"We saved you from grave harm last night," Mother Leviticus reminded me with a crocodile's smile. "The least you could do is hear what I have to say, no?"

Seeing as I still didn't have any of my things, or even know where I was, I didn't seem to have an awful lot of choice. And I sincerely doubted that Mother Leviticus would make things easy for me if I ran out. They'd already locked me up once, after all, and I was in no condition to defend myself.

I sunk back into my chair, and her grin widened.

"Something you've told our Father," she said, "is that you didn't think you could ever be admitted into Heaven."

Saying nothing, I only watched her, unblinking, waiting for her to get to the point.

"So what if I told you that we can change that?" She paused, observing me expectantly, probably hoping that my expression would brighten up or I'd say something, but I didn't do her that favor. I kept my face unimpressed, waiting.

A smirk perked up her lips. "My, I'd almost believe I'm dealing with a non-believer! Why, haven't you yourself experienced the tremendous forces? Haven't you *seen* a demon's power? If *they* are our Lord's adversaries, how much more powerful do you imagine God to be? Do you doubt that He can change your fate?"

She wanted me to react, to speak, admit to something, that much was clear. I couldn't hope for a lie to hold, so I chose to say nothing.

Her hand reached across the table to stroke mine and her smirk was replaced by a compassionate frown. "Amelia… We know that you have gone astray. We know a demon has coerced you into binding your soul to him, but believe in the shepherd. He will guide you back on the right path. He will forgive you, and He will free you."

It was hard not to roll my eyes at her speech. It seemed like a caricature, so ridiculous, and above all, I wasn't sure how much of her own words she believed in. How much of it was only said to win me over?

Finally, I decided it was time to speak up. "What do you want?"

Mother Leviticus relaxed in her seat, her pleased and relaxed expression a sign she was seemingly convinced that she had won this battle. Maybe I should've stayed quiet after all.

"As you may have surmised, we are a Holy Order. We've been tasked by the Lord himself to banish demons from this plane. Exorcise them, if you will. To truly protect humanity, however, we need to eradicate evil itself. The root of the original sin — the snake that came to the garden and poisoned the mind of our ancestors. The Order has tirelessly worked toward this goal for centuries — millennia, even — but never have we had as good a chance as we do now."

My brows furrowed into a frown. I was bait.

Still, I played dumb. "And what do I have to do with all of that?" I asked.

Mother Leviticus's smile broadened, as though she had waited for this question to be asked. "This demon appears to be somewhat *attached* to you. We tried to prevent it from going that far, of course. That's why Father Exodus approached you in the first place, but clearly, his efforts did not bear fruit, pardon the joke. However, your case appears to be different to previous observations we made about those who'd entered a pact. For some reason, the demon appears to be somewhat... forgive my repetition... attached to you."

Yup, I was a worm, wriggling on a hook that was about to be thrown in the water.

My frown had become a glare before I'd known what was happening.

"This is where our offer comes in," she went on. "If you can help us get to the demon, we can make sure your soul will ascend to Heaven after all."

She had no such power, and we both knew it. The

dead-fish look in her eyes told me as much. But she believed that I might fall for her words. I tried to think quickly, doing my best to figure out what the best way forward was. If I refused, I expected that I'd be locked up again or worse and be used as bait anyway. Even though they called themselves a "holy order" I somehow didn't doubt that they went to drastic measures that were anything but holy to achieve their goals.

The ends justify the means.

I could lie. I could pretend to agree and secretly plan to warn Luce. It would gain me a certain amount of autonomy, I could imagine. But I just didn't want to. Every fiber of my being refused to volunteer to throw Luce in front of the bus, even if it was only pretense. He'd helped me so many times. He was my *friend.* He wasn't evil, he didn't try to coerce people into doing evil things, either. He believed in freedom, in choice. And so I made mine.

"I can't help you," I said, holding my head up high and looking straight at Mother Leviticus. "And you couldn't possibly help me, either. And you know what? I don't want you to. I know what choices I made, and I stand by them. I'm certain that Eve did, too."

A spark of anger flashed across her otherwise composed expression when I mentioned Eve, but it was gone before I could fully register it.

"You must still be confused from your injuries,"

she said smoothly, smiling. "Father Exodus, would you be so kind to escort Mrs. Perez to her room so she may rest?"

"Ms.," I corrected her and then I chuckled to myself. It really was like a compulsion, wasn't it? I stood up and left the room.

"Amy." David hurried after me, grabbing my wrist.

I turned to him only long enough to jerk my hand free, despite the flash of pain it induced in my shoulder. "Save it."

I walked on, back the way to my windowless prison cell. I considered escaping but set the idea aside quickly. What would be the point? In my state, I wouldn't make it very far. And truth be told, I relished the thought of being able to just lie down for a few days until everything stopped aching. Though a window would be nice. And a non-religious book to read. Maybe even a kitchen for some baking. I could always escape once my body no longer screamed at me for breathing.

"I just want to apologize." David fell in step beside me. I wasn't exactly able to move fast enough to run away or anything, but I refused to look at him.

"And I just don't care if you do."

"What about giving you an explanation, at least?"

Now that was more interesting. As angry as I was at him, I was also incredibly curious how everything slotted together. I stopped my snail stride for a moment to grant him a look after all. "That, I'll take."

Chapter 13

Half an hour later, David entered my new room—one that at least had a window, even though it was barred with a metal grate and only opened into the courtyard—carrying a tray of small sandwiches and juice. I was sitting propped up on the bed, resting my body and hoping that the throbbing pain would fade soon. Setting down the tray on the small nightstand beside me, he pulled up a stool from the wall to sit beside me once the door had fallen into its lock. Though the sandwiches looked delicious, cream cheese and salmon amongst other things, I didn't touch them. Not yet.

"Well?" I asked, raising an eyebrow after an extended period of awkward silence.

He fidgeted a little, avoiding my gaze, a pained expression on his face. "Well, I'm sure you can guess some parts at least—"

"Assume that I can't and tell me anyway." I interrupted him with a steely gaze. "And spare no detail."

"Well..." He rubbed the back of his neck awkwardly. "I've been a part of this organization my whole life. You could call it a family tradition."

"So Kit is part of it as well?"

He nodded. "A few weeks ago, we received some reports that suggested that there might be some demonic activity going on in the area, and when we investigated, we realized that there was a high chance of you having been in contact with a demon. But we didn't know how far along that contact was yet—if it was just a demon observing you, if it was out for a pact, or if it intended to devour you whole. We couldn't intervene without knowing more, without knowing how much you might know, so after our usual tactics didn't work, we decided to try the personal approach and sent Kit in to create a connection."

He paused and I mulled over his words for a moment. What a great job Kit had done. Truly. We'd become such fast friends in no time. A plus.

"But by then you and I had already spoken on the phone. You made a connection. Why get her to introduce us?"

He shrugged.

"The phone wasn't enough. It wasn't the kind of connection that would make you open doors. We needed even a tangential connection to you so you'd let your guard down. Kit was watching you before and… you don't seem to respond all that well to complete strangers."

He must be referring to that night Luce and I had

danced in the club that Kit had apparently observed.

My eyes narrowed as I glared at him. "So you tricked me into liking you?" My voice was cold, and any affection or infatuation I might have been feeling for him up until that point wholly dissipated as if it had never been there to begin with.

He cast down his eyes, unable to withhold my stare. "I followed orders."

I snorted. "Orders, huh? What else were you ordered to do? Break into my house?"

He didn't answer and my blood froze.

"You did, didn't you?" I already knew the answer. Had suspected it before I'd known Father Exodus and David were the same person. "You actually broke into my house. And then after that, you called me as if nothing had happened."

He didn't deny it. He didn't confirm it either, but his lips parted slightly, as though he were planning on saying something before something in my eyes convinced him to stay quiet. It was far more than an admission of guilt.

I shook my head, exasperated, remembering how scared I'd been, how violated I'd felt, now knowing exactly to what degree I had truly been wronged.

"When you gasped on the phone and then went quiet, I was worried something had happened." David continued on, though he stared down at his hands. "So I came running over. I thought maybe the demon had finally made his appearance and I wanted to protect you. But then when you opened the door, I could smell the sulfur, and the demon was there, so I finally had the proof and information I needed. So I returned here, getting everything ready to deal with it. Kit was keeping an eye on you during that time, and she detected continuous traces of Hell's presence on you, which told us that for some reason, the demon must be coming back over and over. This is unheard of. Demons make their deals and then they disappear. There's never been a case like yours before."

"My, I'm honored," I responded dryly. "Then what?"

He rubbed a hand over his face. "Well, we were always going to ask for your cooperation. It was pure chance that it happened to be the same evening when I'd see two demons fight over you." Finally, he looked up at me again, a confused frown making his brows almost touch. "Why are they?"

I shrugged uncomfortably. "Heck if I know," I mumbled, worry about Luce once more returning to my mind. How powerful was Paimon? How strong? And on that note, how did their strength compare, typically? And why hadn't Luce shown up yet to make sure I was okay? Admittedly, I should have been glad about it, since this was a trap for him and all, but I was also feeling a little hurt that he hadn't so much as checked in. He *had* seen me get hurt, after all. So much so that it had lit a fire under him.

But he wasn't here. And that worried me. For all the Order knew, their job had already been finished by someone else. Although... David kept saying *demon* instead of *Devil*, which led me to believe that, perhaps, they didn't actually know that I'd made my deal with Lucifer himself.

David watched me for a moment longer before sighing. He took my hand, a pained expression crossing his face. "We just want to help you. We really do. You don't have to go to Hell. You don't have to resign yourself to that kind of fate. If we can defeat the demon, you're free."

He squeezed my hand, and I raised an eyebrow. "What makes you think I want that?"

"What?" He recoiled, shaking his head. "What are you talking about? You could be *free*. You could be welcomed back to paradise!"

I smiled wryly. "I *am* free. I was free to make my choice. And I don't regret it."

David shook his head desperately and grabbed my shoulder. "This isn't true; it's the demon talking. He's seduced you, tempted you. Don't let him win. You can fight it. I know you can, Amelia. You want to go to Heaven. We all do. And you deserve to. You just need to resist the demon's voice."

My voice was icy when I spoke again. "Don't presume to make my choices for me, David. I'm very much capable of doing that myself. The *demon* fulfilled a wish I had. He didn't talk me into it. I've never met a man who's respected my wishes more than he has, without question."

"No, listen. God will forgive you if you just—"

"No, *you* listen. I don't give a rat's ass about God's forgiveness. If he scorns me for making my own choices and following my own beliefs and rationale, then he's no better than any mortal jerk and I couldn't care less about getting into his *paradise*. Give me Hell any day. At least I know that it's ruled by someone who sees me as a person who deserves respect."

My body might have been worn down, and I might have been imprisoned here, but I held my head high as I gave David a piece of my mind. Righteous energy flowed through my veins, and I never felt more at peace and powerful than I did right then.

"I would never help you to hurt him." Warmth filled my body at the thought of Luce. "Because he's my friend."

I felt strong and confident, relaxed, even, but David only shook his head sadly.

"I can see that his hold over you is too strong." He took my hand and smiled empathetically. "But don't worry. We will bring you salvation."

He left.

Staring at the door he'd locked after leaving for a few moments, I tried to understand how someone could be listening so attentively and yet not hear a word of what I said. He thought I was the one being manipulated, but he was the one acting brainwashed.

So what now?

There was no way out of this room, and even if I could pry the grate away from the window, I was in far too much pain to climb down a wall—never mind that I wasn't even certain I would have been capable of it at peak health, either. It always looked so easy and straightforward in movies, but I knew I didn't have the strength for it, not exactly being the fittest person around.

I decided to have a nap instead. With any luck, the world would look different when I awoke again. Whether that meant my pain would be gone, or I'd be home, or Luce was here… I'd take any option, really.

I opened my eyes to find Kit sitting by the bedside, reading a book. She looked completely different than she ever had at the office. For one thing, her face lacked any and all expression. But her outfit was different, too. Instead of her usual frilly, pastel-colored clothes, she now wore a pair of jeans along with a simple grey T-shirt, and black combat boots that she had propped up on the side of the bed. Her hair was tied back; no more were the playful curls framing her face. Even though she'd only changed her outfit, her whole demeanor had seemingly changed alongside it from a ditzy, ignorant young woman, to a badass. Looking at her like this, I didn't doubt her ability to knock me out in a fight. Strange how such a small change could make all the difference in how I saw someone.

"Um…" I propped myself up. "Hi, Kit."

She looked up from her book, her cool gaze resting on me before an uncharacteristic, snarky smirk snuck onto her red lips. "Oh, look. Our little demon-lover is finally awake."

Damn, she was like a whole other person. Even her voice sounded different. It had lost its childlike, insolent quality and now dripped with confidence. And I was pretty sure I could also detect a few not-very-subtle hints of disdain in her demeanor. Wow. I really wouldn't have taken her for that good an actress. I'd been wholly taken in.

"Follow me." Without checking to see if I actually followed, Kit jumped to her feet, and strode out of the room. I scrambled out of bed, flinching when dull pain throbbed throughout my body, and followed as quickly as I could without falling over, which, admittedly, was pretty slow. By the time I'd made it to the door, she was already at the end of the hallway, her ponytail swinging from side to side. She wasn't even so much as looking back for me. Great. Apparently, some things didn't change.

I clenched my teeth and hurried after her so that

the distance between us at least wouldn't get any larger. Even though this could have been the perfect opportunity to look for my stuff, or at least a phone of sorts, and escape, I was too curious about what Kit had to show me. Besides, I didn't feel like I was in any danger, and they knew where I lived and worked, anyway. They probably knew all about Lynn as well. So where was I gonna go? The cops? Yeah, right.

"So, Mrs. Perez."

"Ms."

"Ms. Perez... You say you were kidnapped by a religious cult that held you hostage to... lure out the Devil? Whom you claim is your best friend? Please come with us for a moment. These are our specialists who would like to have a conversation with you. Don't mind the white jackets. And don't worry about the restraints, either. They are purely there for your own safety."

Yup, that would go over *so* well.

Following Kit, I stubbed my toe multiple times, once so hard that it continued to ache with every step. Fantastic. I supposed could add a broken toe to the seemingly ever-growing list of my injuries. Reaching the bottom of a spiral staircase, I saw Kit's hair disappear around a corner up ahead, but by the time I got there, she was gone again. I tentatively kept walking, looking all around for her. It was a ground-level hallway with continuous stone arches opening into the courtyard on the right wall. As above, it was completely made from stone, simple yet somewhat imposing. Like in the hallway my room was located on, a stretch of closed doors were lined along the left side of the hall. Even though it was a straight and quite long hallway, Kit had somehow evaporated. I hadn't thought that I'd been lagging that much behind, but unless she'd ducked into one of the rooms and shut the door or leapt through one of the open archways into the courtyard, I couldn't tell how she'd managed her vanishing act.

A little confused, I walked on, at a slower pace now that I wasn't trying to keep up with a sprinting maniac anymore. If nothing else, at least I finally had the opportunity to take a look around the place and get my bearings, perhaps even figure out just how far away from town I was. Who knew—maybe I could even find a car that I could use to hightail it outta here?

Like before, the courtyard was full of people in habits milling about busily. Only a few of them noticed me in the hallway, and their gazes were a mixture of disdain and pity, as if I were roadkill. Still, unlike what I'd expected, none of them made a move to stop me from wandering about. They looked at me, and then they went back about their business. I supposed that as long as I wasn't actively summoning Luce for them, I wasn't considered a threat, or of use, or much of anything, really.

I got to the end of the hallway, where it split into two more hallways, one to the left, farther into the building, and one to the right around the courtyard. I decided to go left, if only to escape the glares. Besides, having seen practically nothing of the place, I was curious as to what else I might find.

The hallway was lit up by LED lights, bright and steady, and absolutely not what I would have expected to find in a place like this. Candles and torches, sure. Heck, even flickering halogen lights would have fit my expectations better. Even cults followed the times, didn't they?

Along this hallway were a few open doorways and I made a point of peeking through each one of them. There was a small cabinet where cleaning supplies were kept, including some pretty aggressive bleach that I would have expected to eat right through this type of stone; there was another small, windowless storage room where preserves and other bottled and canned goods were stacked on shelves; and there was a small office space that reminded me a lot of the one Mother Leviticus used. The room's occupant must have just stepped out a moment ago, based on the still-steaming cup of coffee on the table beside an opened laptop. Glancing up and down the hallway, I contemplated whether or not it would be worth it to try and send out an email to someone, just to alert anyone of my position, even if it was only to inform my boss that I wouldn't be able to come into work tomorrow.

Well, it probably wouldn't hurt.

I slipped into the room, leaving the door open so I could hear if anyone were to approach, and skirted around the desk to the laptop. Pursing my lips, I glared at the locked screen. Why did it have to be password protected? And without any hint that might help me?

Halfheartedly, I decided to give it a shot anyway, since I was already here.

First, I tried the name of the order: *Ordo Sancti Matrem Suam.*

No dice.

I stared at the screen, wondering what other obvious passwords I could try. Pressing *enter* without typing anything also didn't work. My final attempt was simply to type *God.* Sure, it was a long shot, but hey, better try and fail than not try at all, right?

Sadly, everything I tried was a complete and utter bust. I remembered Amanda showing me a trick at work a while back—a way to change a user's password without having to know the original one. She'd have no problems dealing with this, but I was stuck. As much as I tried, I couldn't recall just how she'd done it when she'd shown me. In my defense, it wasn't a skill I needed very often. Or ever.

Giving up on the computer, I decided to look around the office instead. You never knew if you might find something of use lying around. The desk drawers were empty, with the exception of a jelly donut and the shelves along the wall only held a large number of files. They were named after people and places, and obviously, I checked if I happened to see something that matched my own profile, but no luck there, either. This place was completely and utterly useless.

Stepping out of the room, I spotted movement at the end of the hallway and hurried toward it. I passed through a heavy, undecorated wooden door that was braced with steel bands, only to end up in a large cathedral-like hall with stained-glass windows high up, and many bare benches arranged in a circle around a small podium beside a cross. Pillars were masoned to look like demons and angels engaged in (im)mortal combat, while frescos along the walls depicted more of the same kind of scenes as those in the smaller cathedral.

Two masoned depictions in the walls especially stuck out to me, east and west of the podium. The one to the west portrayed a man and a woman in the desert wearing nothing but fig leaves over their private parts fighting a snake bearing its venomous fangs. A half-eaten apple core lay on the ground between them, tainting the earth they stood on with a spreading shadow. Behind them was an oasis, but it was set ablaze, a smoking torch still held by the snake's tail.

The one to the east showed a young mother, clad in simple clothing, her infant child clutched to her chest with one arm, away from the ravenous goat-demon, kept at bay with the sword she wielded with her other hand. The masonry was excellently done. I could see the fear and determination in her expression as clearly as if she were standing before me in the flesh.

I slowly walked around the podium, looking at all the different vivid frescos and masonry around, until I tripped, stubbing my toe once more with a yelp. Annoyed, I looked down at what had brought me pain and found steps. Steps that were leading down, underneath the cross and into flickering light. Torches.

Suspecting that the movement I'd seen earlier had come from whoever had opened this and lit the torches, I found it difficult to resist my curiosity. Besides, with any luck, this led down into some secret underground garage full of Batmobiles. Before I had even made the conscious decision, I was heading down the bare stone steps. They weren't nearly as well-worn as the rest of the abbey's floors appeared to be; the stone was still much coarser on my bare feet. I followed down the spiral staircase, much farther than I had expected, and with every step I took, the air got colder, stuffier, and moldier. I glanced back up, nervously hoping to still see the opening, but I'd already gone several rounds around the staircase. The only things illuminating my surroundings were the lit torches along the walls.

Now *this* was what I had expected a cult's home to look like. After another two or three minutes, I finally reached the next level, and even though the stairs led farther into the ground, the torches were only lit to this point. I found myself in an arched hallway that directed me toward a larger cave. Determined, I snuck toward it, making sure I was making as little sound as possible, so as not to alert anyone of my presence, just in case.

"Took you long enough."

Kit's voice made me flinch, and I whirled around to her. She emerged from a shadowy nook in the wall, one eyebrow arched and a disapproving pout on her lips.

She sighed. "Must be the old age."

Rude!

"Or my injuries, maybe?" I frowned at her, but she only shrugged and pushed past me, toward the cave.

"Just hurry it up."

Frustrated though I was, I bit back my snarky reply and followed into the cavern.

The room was just about high enough for me to stand upright, but if I'd been only a little taller, I'd be hitting my head constantly on the uneven ceiling. It was a very wide space, with twelve pillars holding up the ceiling and a statue in the center of the room. The walls had little nooks with portraits of people and candles lit in front of them.

I was starting to wonder how there was still enough oxygen to breathe down here without carbon monoxide poisoning, considering all the open flames. Did they have an air vent somewhere? I wouldn't put it past them.

"Take a look around," Kit said, leaning against the wall, pushing against it with one boot. Sounds were a little muffled in this space and the moist smell was penetrant enough to make it difficult to breathe deeply, but I nodded and started my round, even though coldness was seeping into my bare feet.

I went around from nook to nook, looking at the pictures, reading the inscribed names in the stone, along with their dates of birth and death. There were probably around fifty or sixty people named down here, a lot of whom shared last names. There were the Holleys, the Tripstons, the Buckleys, and the Millers. Those were the most common ones, anyway. There were some others as well, but they usually only appeared once or twice. There was a relatively even spread between male and female, and their relation couldn't be denied, not considering how much their images resembled one another. Most of them seemed to have their images taken some time between the ages of twenty-five and forty, but I did see one or two teenagers, and even a baby among them.

After I'd rounded about half of the nooks, I realized something they all had in common — not one of them seemed to have lived past forty, and a noteworthy number of them had actually died *on* their fortieth birthday. I shuddered when I considered the implications. I didn't really understand what it meant, or what Kit wanted me to see, but the creepiness factor rose with every name and date I saw.

Every photo showed me a person with a hard edge to their gaze, like they were determined to succeed or die trying. Evidently, the latter had occurred, or why else would they have been down here in a crypt in some cultish abbey?

When I'd finished my circle, blood draining further from my face with every step, I glanced at Kit. She only nudged her chin to the statue in the center, and, obediently, I went closer to take a look.

I first noticed the twelve pillars not being as straightforward as they'd seemed from a distance. No, they all had carvings in them. Not professional masonry like in the hall above, but rather, crude carvings that had clearly been added at a later date by laymen. They weren't etched into the stone very deeply, and time had eroded some, so it was hard to make out what exactly they looked like in the flickering candle light, but I got the gist of it based on all the other things I'd seen. More imagery of people fighting the Devil and his army of demons. I let my fingers gently pass over one of the carvings, as if I were hoping that I'd be able to make it out better by touch.

Then I diverted my attention to the statue in the center of the room. It was sitting at the head of a sort of sarcophagus, reaching from the floor up to the ceiling, almost like a thirteenth column.

Now that I was getting a closer look at it, I could tell it was actually made up of three parts, three distinct figures. And I recognized two of them. I'd seen them both before, years ago, though Luce had done a good job not letting them peek out since then. His Devil shape was holding on to a young woman, dragging her down into the flames of Hell. But she, with tears in her eyes, was reaching out to his angelic counterpart, terrifying though it was in its accuracy. I shuddered, seeing these representations of Luce down here in this crypt. What did it mean? Someone along the way must have seen both of Luce's shapes, that much was clear. But why? Under what circumstances? Their meaning in this scene, in this place, was also lost on me for the moment. My gaze went down and found a name etched into the sarcophagus. Meredith Holley. There were no dates beneath her name.

Muffled steps approached from behind, and Kit stopped next to me.

"The Devil seduced her," she said quietly, icily, glaring at the statue. "He tempted her into making a deal with him. But it was a deal that cost not only her soul, but those of all her descendants as well. We were lucky for her friendship with an angel." Her eyes softened a little as her gaze moved from Luce's Devil shape to his other one. "While he couldn't erase the deal completely, he could lessen the effects, so that while all Meredith's descendants would still die by the time they reached forty, their souls would not belong to the Devil, but instead be sent to the Heavens, so long as they fought for righteousness and never invited Evil into their lives." She gestured in a slow semi-circle to the room at large. "All these are those who fought the curse, who fought righteously and still had to die young."

I remained quiet, and not only because I didn't want to point out that the angel and Devil depicted were the same individual. Would Luce really have made such a deal? Yes, he'd asked for my soul as payment when it had come to our deal, but I couldn't imagine him asking for those of my descendants. It didn't sound like him, but being here, seeing that none of these people had lived past their cursed age, and seeing Kit, so convinced by all of it, by the curse that I surmised affected her as well, it was enough to give me pause.

"The curse won't be broken until the Devil is destroyed." She now looked at me directly, her determined gaze drilling into mine. I wouldn't have been surprised to see her eyes spark. They were drenched with need and resignation alike.

This is her destiny, I thought. *Or at least what she*

thinks her destiny is.

"Knowing this, can you really call a demon your *friend*? Are you naïve enough to trust that it won't betray you? That it really was worth it, selling your soul to it?"

With every question, she stepped closer to me, and I edged away until one of the pillars was hindering my path.

Kit glared at me for a moment longer, inches away from me, before sidestepping and heading out. "That's all I had to say."

Chapter 19

I remained in the crypt a little while longer, looking at the images, at the statue, at the inscriptions, wondering what was real and what wasn't. I was certain that the Luce I knew wouldn't do what Kit had told me, so the real question was whether that was because he'd changed, or because there'd been some misunderstanding.

I tried to separate the facts I believed from the ones I was uncertain about or knew to be untrue.

I believed that Meredith probably had made a deal with Luce, and that he had granted it. I also believed that each one of the people immortalized in this room had died before the completion of their fortieth birthday (which briefly made me wonder how that would fare for someone born on the twenty-ninth of February until I remembered that forty is a duplicate of the four-year-gap). It was pretty obvious that for some reason, both of Luce's shapes came into play, and that none of Meredith's descendants had realized that they were both him. Or at least, no one here knew. Kit's gaze had been full of scorn when directed at Devil Luce, but it had softened slightly when she'd looked at Angel Luce.

What I didn't believe in the slightest was the curse business. Sure, something was fishy about it, but I honestly couldn't imagine that Luce was capable of cursing a whole family line. I could be wrong, of course, but from what I knew, all of his deals, and the corresponding payment, accumulated to a debt that only the person making the deal could pay. He was all about choice, so cursing people for something they'd had no part in seemed uncharacteristic. But what else could be causing these people to die young?

Judging by the way Kit had spoken about it, there didn't seem to be any exceptions, even of people who might not be documented in this room. It seemed like the kind of thing the family would be keen to keep a close eye on. There was a connection to what had happened between Meredith and Luce, I could feel it, but as to what it was, I could only take a guess. Perhaps it had been Meredith herself who had willingly cursed her descendants. But would Luce have accepted such a deal? Truthfully, I didn't know enough about the rules for his deals to be sure, so while I didn't *think* he would, or even could, I had zero proof to back that up.

Eventually, after contemplating Kit's family history for a long time, the cold creeping into my bones became too much, and I headed back upstairs, leaving the torches and candles burning. For a moment while heading up the staircase, I worried I would find the door closed and myself entombed, but I breathed out a sigh of relief when I found it open. I climbed out, looking around for Kit, but she was long gone.

I walked back the way I had come, though the office I'd peeked into earlier was shut now. I contemplated briefly whether or not I should continue my search for a vehicle that could carry me away, but Mother Leviticus, accompanied by two acolytes, found me by the time I reached the courtyard. Her eyes narrowed.

"Who unlocked your room?" she demanded to know. Wow, okay. Apparently, I wasn't even worth so much as a "hello."

"Isn't it a lovely day for a stroll?" I exclaimed, beaming back at her. I could play stupid and naïve. She absolutely didn't make me want to show her any real side of me.

Her face softened and she actually smiled, though it didn't reach her eyes. "Say, dear, aren't you cold, only wearing that? And how are your injuries?"

She'd got me there. I was freezing. The cold of the crypt nestled in my bones, and it certainly hadn't helped me ache any less. If anything, it had made things worse.

"It's okay," I lied, smiling halfheartedly.

"I must insist you get some bed rest," Mother Leviticus said, giving her companions a subtle order with her hand and they stepped to either side of me, as if to prop me up to help, though I felt more like I was a prisoner being led away. "As long as you are our guest, I would hate for any harm to befall you, so please, allow us to look after your wellbeing."

She nodded to the acolytes, and they marched me right back to my room, though at least at a slow pace that wasn't too taxing. Funny how such kind words could feel so threatening.

I started reading the Bible Kit had left in my room after I'd gotten bored of hearing my own thoughts echo around my head once too many times. Even though it wasn't exactly my literature of choice, it was better than having nothing at all for distraction.

I had nothing else to occupy myself except for the two meager meals a day that were brought in by silent nuns, and letting my thoughts wander whenever I wasn't reading, eating, or sleeping. Seeing as my door was locked at almost all times, I sure was glad that I'd been relocated to a room with a window and on-suite bathroom. Surprisingly, I got a lot more enjoyment out of staring out the window into the courtyard for long periods of time than I'd thought I would.

After two days, as I was just beginning to wonder how soon anyone at home would miss me and perhaps start asking questions, David came by to visit.

"How are you feeling?" he asked as he entered the room, a crooked grin telling me he already knew the answer.

"Peachy," I snapped. "I love being locked up by overzealous religious folks. It's every girl's dream and aspiration—didn't you know?"

He closed the door behind him and sat down on the foot of my bed while I leaned against the window.

"That's fair." He sighed and ran his fingers through his hair. "But you do understand why, don't you? Kit told me she showed you our… history."

I softened a little upon seeing his expression. His brows were furrowed as he looked down at his fumbling hands instead of me.

"I have some questions," I said after a moment. Feeling bad for the guy, I walked over to take a seat next to him.

David looked up at me, almost surprised, and he nodded quickly.

"I'll be happy to answer whatever I can." A frown crossed his face. "But before we get to that—how are you feeling, really? Are you still hurting?"

I rolled my shoulder a little to loosen the tender flesh where Paimon had bit into me. It seemed like years had passed since then, even though it hadn't even been a week yet.

"Yeah," I admitted. "But it's getting better."

Luckily, it seemed that my ribs hadn't been broken after all, only bruised. And while those bruises still remained, coloring more every day, the pain was lessening slowly, though I was by no means back to my old self.

The thought of Paimon brought back other questions. This cult was heavily focused on Luce, but how much did they know about the Kings of Hell? Did they know anything about them at all? And if they didn't, should I mention them? David had witnessed the fight between Luce and Paimon, so he must have some idea, especially since he hadn't brought it up.

Still, other questions were more pressing on my mind.

"So, how is your family connected to this place?" I gestured at the walls. "I mean, Kit said that you had to fight righteously or whatever, but how does that translate to this, exactly?"

He granted me another crooked smile.

"The order is much older than the curse. But it used to be more passive. It was full of old, stuffy men who thought they could pray the Devil away. It was Catherine Holley who changed all that."

I tried to remember if I'd read that name in the crypt, but there'd been so many names, it was hard to recollect any of them except Meredith's.

"She was Meredith's younger sister, and she was

the only one who noticed the Devil and the angel's interactions with Meredith. See, Meredith was known as a kind and charitable woman who always did her best to help her community and do what was right. But Catherine saw the Devil whisper into her ear. She saw her sister fall for his schemes and remained powerless because she was so much younger. She also saw the angel comforting Meredith. But then, later, long after she saw her sister die, Catherine witnessed the effects of the curse on Meredith's children, and she made a vow to help them break it. She sought out the order, entered, and rose to power, changing its structure so it could become the shelter for her sister's children and their children, helping them seek out the Devil to destroy him. We became exterminators for anything from Hell."

I shuddered. How many demons had they faced? How many demons had they been able to kill, or been killed by? And most importantly, how long had it taken David to learn this speech of his by heart? Because the phrasing he used simply oozed repetition.

"What about her? Catherine, I mean."

David shrugged. "She wasn't affected by the curse because she wasn't one of Meredith's descendants, but she became Mother Superior and guided several generations into battle. It became her life's mission."

All of this had started with one person who'd

wanted to undo what her sister had caused. Knowing from personal experience, I was perfectly aware that no one except the person making the deal with Luce could hear the terms of it. It wasn't something that was spoken aloud, or something physical to sign. It was more like for a moment, your consciousness merged with Luce's, and you understood one another fully, he understood exactly what it was you wanted, and you knew fully what you were giving up in exchange. There was no room for ambiguity. And equally, no one outside of the deal could be a part of it. So how had Catherine pieced together the information? How much of it had been speculation, assumption, perhaps even misunderstanding?

"If you don't mind my asking," I began hesitantly, "how does the 'curse' come into effect?"

David got up and walked to the window, his brows tightly knit together, his lips twitching. It must have been hard for him to speak about it. It wasn't like it didn't affect him, after all. I mean, his fortieth birthday couldn't have been that far away. He must have been in his mid-thirties. His younger cousin Kit had a lot more time left.

He rested one arm on the wall above the window, peering into the courtyard, as if he was hoping to find the answer there. He watched the acolytes hurry about, and I, in turn, watched him. For several minutes, not a sound echoed through the room.

Then, finally, just as I started to consider retracting my question, David sighed.

"None of us can live past forty, that much we know. It's been proven, over and over again. Unless something causes us to die first, like an illness, or an accident, every member of my family is found dead the day after their fortieth birthday. It..." He shuddered. "It always looks like suicide."

He pressed his eyes shut and gulped. Was he remembering an instance when he'd found someone dead? Perhaps a parent or elder sibling? I didn't dare ask.

But it still didn't make any sense. Luce couldn't control people's actions. At least not any more than any other human manipulator.

"But thanks to the angel, as long as we fight righteously, we're not doomed to go to Hell."

His gaze returned to me, pitying, because my fate was a different one, even though I wasn't the one sure to die within the next five years.

We looked into each other's eyes for a moment. Then he asked, "Why did you do it? What did the demon promise you?"

I contemplated him for a moment, considering telling him the truth. But in the end, I shook my head and smiled, putting a finger to my smiling lips. "I'll never tell. But it was a long time ago."

His eyes widened. "A long time ago? How long?"

"Five years, coming up on six."

His mouth fell open and he stared at me, disbelief written all over his face. I got it. He'd been working under the assumption that he could save me from making a deal in the first place, never knowing that they'd all been years too late for that. Time to tell him that it hadn't just been a random demon, either. With any luck, that'd prove to him that Luce really wasn't as evil as he appeared to think.

"But…" he started and stopped again, trying to reorder his thoughts. I could see the cogs turning in his head, winding around and trying to get things moving. "But the demon, he… And you…?"

I tilted my head to one side, smiling sweetly. "Didn't I say he was my friend?"

"Then… That man, the one fighting the other demon…" Realization was beginning to dawn on him.

I nodded. "That was Luce."

"Luce… *Lucifer*?"

"Yup."

"*The Morningstar*?"

"That's the one."

"But… he was protecting you."

"Because he's my friend," I repeated, more meaningfully, and then I went on, listing things using my fingers to count. "We watch bad movies together, have breakfast together, eat sushi, he sets me up on dates, he comforts me when I have a bad day at work, we go dancing together, he drinks coffee while I have tea… You know, like friends."

"He's the *Devil!*"

"I'm aware."

We looked at one another, I, calmly and somewhat stubbornly, he, with his lips parted, his face pale, and his eyes wide.

Then David turned and left without another word.

You'd think that in the week or so I'd spent locked up in this room, I'd be fretting and angry about my situation, blaming everyone and everything. But honestly, after I'd enjoyed having some peace and quiet and calm for a day or two, I was getting bored. And the boredom was making me anxious. I spent hours just pacing up and down the room, trying to suppress the unsettling feeling in my stomach while studiously avoiding any thoughts pertaining to Lynn's wedding, Luce's wellbeing, and my job. Oh, god, I hoped I wasn't going to get fired for being kidnapped. That would really suck.

The one good thing about being here was that my wounds had gotten a nice start on healing and even my bruising had started to go down. By the end of the week, I still felt some dull aches, and my skin continued to resemble a firework of colorful spectacles, but I mostly felt like a normal human again.

I had started to choreograph a dance for Lynn's wedding in my head, figuring it was at least something to do, when Mother Leviticus came to visit.

I was stretching at the time, hoping to get myself more limber or something before trying out some of the moves — to admittedly very little success — when she opened the door.

"Child," she said coolly. "Have you made up your mind about helping us defeat the demon who deceived you?"

Interesting. She was still calling Luce a "demon." Apparently, David hadn't passed on the newest piece of info I'd shared with him. I sat up straight and shrugged. "Quite a while ago, actually."

"And?"

"I stand by what I said before."

She raised one of her eyebrows. "You still insist that he is your friend, despite the evidence that he does not care enough to come for you here?"

I shrugged again. "It's not like he's my bodyguard. He doesn't have any obligation to just show up, you know. He's my friend, not my dog."

It did worry me, though. Not for my sake — because I figured I was safe, if, however, somewhat inconvenienced — but for his. There had to be a reason he hadn't come, and I saw only three options: He couldn't figure out where I was due to some cult mojo, he thought I was off somewhere having fun with David, or something had happened to stop him. And based on the situation I had last seen him in, I was pretty certain it was the final option, something I didn't like even one bit. Anytime I thought about that, I felt nauseous and like the ground was falling away from underneath my feet. There was, however, a fourth possibility. It was believable that he knew exactly what was going on and would only show up if I actually called for him, which I intentionally hadn't done, not that I really believed it would get through to him.

Mother Leviticus gave me a long, hard stare, her lips pressed together to a thin line. Then she turned and left, David stepping inside to take her place instead. He wordlessly held out a small plastic bag to me.

I took it gingerly and peeked in, only to find my own clothes—washed and mended—along with my phone, purse, and car keys inside. My head shot up to David. "What's this?"

He looked at me, rings under his eyes and the lines deeper than before, making him appear tired and haggard. "I'm taking you home." He nodded to the bag. "I'll give you a few minutes."

Before I could respond, he'd left, closing the door behind him. I stared at it for a moment, wondering how he was feeling. By bringing me home, he would be letting me go, along with accepting that the curse, if such a thing really did exist, probably wouldn't be broken within his lifetime. He didn't have that long left, after all.

I felt guilty, thinking about it, but there was nothing I could do, regardless of whether the curse was real or not, and I didn't believe it was. At least not in the way he and Kit seemed to think it was. But, heck, what did I know? I wasn't affected by it. I wasn't part of their family; I only knew a fraction of their history.

But I believed in Luce. And I trusted my gut feeling. Even if I thought I could, I wouldn't summon him here to meet his end. Not even for David.

After a moment, I pulled myself together and changed my clothing before checking the rest of my belongings. My phone was long dead, not having been charged in over a week, but everything else was there and in order. Admittedly, I couldn't fully remember all the things I'd had with me that day, but everything that should have been there was present and accounted for.

A few minutes passed, and a knock on the door announced David's return.

"I'm ready," I called out and he held open the door for me, allowing me to slip out past him. He didn't say a word as I followed him down into the courtyard where a car was waiting for us. There, he turned to me, a black bandana in his hands.

"Sorry, but… you understand, right?"

I shrugged. It certainly didn't come as a surprise that this weird-ass cult wanted to keep their whereabouts hidden, and honestly, at this point, I was just glad they were bringing me home. I couldn't care less about where these headquarters were located.

I allowed David to put the bandana over my eyes—it was better than getting drugged or knocked out, after all—and let him guide me into the passenger seat of the car. Two car doors were shut, and I heard him rustling in the seat beside me just before the motor started.

We drove for a few minutes before he finally spoke up again.

"I'm really sorry," he said quietly. "You never should have ended up in this position. You deserve better."

It was such a cheesy line, I was at a loss for words. Apparently, he took my silence as encouragement to keep speaking. "I wish I could've returned your soul to you, and that I wouldn't have needed to lie to you. I wish we could…"

"My soul isn't your responsibility." I finally cut in. "I made my choice. And what are you apologizing for, anyway? Sure, I wasn't exactly fond of being kidnapped, but you also got me out of a hairy situation and treated my wounds." I shuddered when I thought what else might have happened to me if I'd been in that parking lot for the remainder of

Paimon and Luce's fight. I hoped my car was still in one piece. "I can't exactly blame you for taking a jump at a chance for something you think might save you and your family."

Only the rumbling of the car answered me. We were driving pretty fast, but I wasn't hearing any sounds of the highway or something of the sort.

"And what do you 'wish we could' anyway?" I muttered, not expecting to be heard over the sound of the engine.

"I wish we could be together." David had spoken almost as quietly as I had, but I heard his voice loud and clear. Strange. Even though he'd lied to me, even though he was part of a cult and had some beliefs I definitely couldn't agree with, I would have expected to feel more when he said something like this. But instead, there was a little uncomfortable tug in my stomach, but nothing more. And that tug informed me very clearly that I did not share that wish. Not anymore.

"I'm sorry," I said. No matter which way he interpreted my words, this should put the matter to rest.

We didn't talk for the remainder of the car ride. The constant rumbling put me to sleep at one point, but when I awoke, we were still driving. Eventually, the car stopped, and David reached over to pull the bandana from my eyes.

"I hope you have a good night," he said, his eyes

like those of a sad puppy. I nodded and got out of the car. He'd pretty much parked right in front of my house, and I headed inside without looking back at him.

Chapter 15

After I'd charged my phone, I found out that not only was tomorrow Monday, but I'd also received a million and one missed calls and texts. Most were from Lynn, but there were also a few from Taylor, Brianna, and my boss, Carol. I had a missed call from my dad, too, and one text from Luce. It was dated from the morning after he and Paimon had shown up on the parking lot.

Saw your friend take you away. Stay safe.

Won't be around for a while. Paimon's raising all hell around here. Lol

I recalled what Paimon had said to Luce that evening.

"I just have to take your place."

Raising all hell, huh? I hoped to the blazes of the fiery pits that he didn't mean that Paimon had started a revolution in Hell to dethrone Luce and take his place.

In order to have me.

Shit.

I wracked my brain trying to think if there was anything I could do but came up with nothing. I couldn't go to Hell, at least not until I died, I assumed, and to be honest, as much as I cared for Luce, dying still wasn't on my to-do list just yet. Besides, what could I do? I was a normal woman who just happened to be friends with the Devil, but it wasn't like I had any special powers unless someone was going to challenge me to a dance off, which, I figured, probably wasn't Hell's preferred method of settling disputes.

Was there something to be said for calling on the Big Guy?

I hadn't prayed in a long time, but my uncle had been religious. And I knew God was real, sort of, at least. In a manner of speaking, he was Luce's father, after all. But did prayers even work? I figured it couldn't do any harm, so I folded my hands and shot a quick request to the Heavens.

"Hey, God, um, I don't call often, but I'm friends with one of your, uh, sons? The Morningstar? You know. Luce. And, uh.... I think he might be in trouble, and I'd really appreciate it if you could do something to help him out. Because I don't know what to do."

I sighed, turning to make tea before I even attempted to think about listening or reading any of Lynn's messages. It was already late afternoon, close to evening, but I could drive over there and talk to her... no, wait. My car was still at the office. I'd have to take a taxi.

Keeping in mind how expensive that would be, I

opted for checking the messages before making a judgement call on that.

Texts first because they were easier.

Hey A, just wanted to check if U figured out flowers for bouquets yet. I'll send U the nr of florist when I get home.

I skipped the next few texts, which I assumed would be mostly about wedding planning.

I'm getting worried. Where r u? I'm assuming u know I came by your work, but they told me u were sick. I kno ur not at home, so what the hell is going on? Are you okay? Please respond!

It didn't take long for Lynn to get worried. Two days and she thought I was avoiding her on purpose. I looked at another one.

Give it to me straight — did you and Lucian elope? I can't get a hold of him any more than you. Please tell me you eloped. Because if you didn't, I'm going to have to assume you two died in some kind of accident, and I REALLY don't want to believe that. Seriously, I'm freaking out! Respond already!

I bit my lip, a queasy feeling expanding in my stomach as I opened another of her texts.

I tried to file a missing person's report today. It didn't go well. PLEASE TELL ME YOU'RE OKAY!

And another one.

Oh my god Amy, please, please, if there is a god, I pray that he makes sure you're okay. I don't know what to do anymore. I've tried everything I could think of! I even called your abuela! AND your dad! I've been coming by your house every day and even your neighbors haven't seen you… Why does no one know where you are? What happened?? Please, please respond. Any sign!!!!!!!!!! Please!!!!!!!??!

I put the phone down. I couldn't read any more of her texts, if only because tears were making my vision somewhat blurry. No, calling her would not be enough. I needed to go over. I owed her that much at least. Over the time I'd been looking at her texts—my tea forgotten—my phone had charged enough it should last an hour or two at least, so I unplugged it and headed toward the front door once more, only thinking of how I needed to go see her. But as I opened the door, I found Lynn standing in front of it, her face pale, her eyes red.

We stared at each other for a moment before I wrapped my arms around her, holding her tightly, trying to soothe her shaking body.

"Amy," she whispered, her voice heavy and hoarse with tears. Her nails dug into my clothing as if she needed to reassure herself that I was really there, which was probably not far off the truth.

Without a word, I gently pulled her into the house and closed the door.

"It's okay," I said quietly. "I promise. I'm back now, and I'm not going anywhere." *I hope.*

I guided her to the living room, and we sank into the couch, her hands still wrapped around parts of my shirt. She finally pulled back and looked me over, but when she noticed the bandage around my shoulder peeking out from under my T-shirt and the millions of green and purple marks scattered across my body, she fell right back into sobbing, her hands gently running over my bruises and wrapping.

"Hey, it's okay," I repeated gently, stroking her back. "I'm fine, I promise. Some stuff happened, but I'm back now. And it's okay."

It took a while, but finally, Lynn's sobs subsided, and she could breathe normally again and look at me without sobs shaking her body.

Her lips were still trembling when she asked me the vital question. "What the *hell* happened?"

Her chin jutted forward and her hands shaped into fists, even Lynn's eyes were blazing with anger now, though it didn't seem to be directed at me.

I sighed. "I think we need tea for this conversation. It might be difficult to believe."

I headed to the kitchen, Lynn following closely.

Truthfully, right now, I was glad that Luce wasn't around because if he were, I wouldn't be able to abridge the truth in the way I needed to. No way could I tell Lynn about Luce's real identity. Or about Paimon for that matter. So I needed to change the facts just a little, smudge the edges to turn my past week into a thing of possibility, though even then, it would be a stretch to believe.

We didn't speak while I was boiling the water. Lynn probably couldn't figure out what to say, and I was trying to sort out my thoughts so I didn't say anything that I shouldn't. But finally, we, along with the tea, were ready.

"I… had a stalker," I said. "It's been going on for a few weeks, but it didn't seem like anything to worry about at first. But then last week he ambushed me after work, in the parking lot. And he attacked me."

Lynn gasped, and her gaze flitted to the bandage. No doubt she assumed that I'd been stabbed or shot.

"Luce came to my rescue," I continued, "and they got into a fight. But by then, I was already in… bad shape."

I ran my left hand slowly over the bruises on my right arm, looking at them with a frown. This was where the tough part to believe was coming in.

"And while they were busy, I was kidnapped." I took a deep breath. "By David."

Lynn blinked in confusion. I could see the suspension of disbelief was getting thin, but she didn't interrupt me, so I continued.

"As it turns out, he belongs to some weird religious sect, and they looked after my injuries but also kept me locked up for a week."

I watched Lynn, trying to gage her reaction. I hadn't lied yet, but I wondered how much of this she would believe. She gulped, watching me in turn. Perhaps she was comparing her own fears with realities, or she was trying to determine what was more likely: that I'd come up with such a bad lie to cover up something else, or that it had actually happened. I didn't know for certain what conclusion she came to, but she reached out again, brushing over my bruises.

"What did they want from you?" she asked quietly.

"To join them," I said, which, technically, also wasn't a lie. They wanted me to join forces with them, after all. To aid them to achieve their goal.

She shook her head, as if trying to dispel her confusion.

"But why kidnap you? And wasn't David the cousin of your colleague?"

"Well," I said slowly, "he *did* get me out of danger. I do kind of think his main intention was to get someone to look at my injuries and get me away from the fight. He just… picked his cult instead of a hospital. And once I was there… You know." I shrugged. "And yeah. Kit. Turns out she's a member of the cult, too. Probably why my work thought I was sick."

"This is insane." She ran her fingers through her hair.

"I know."

Then a thought occurred to her. "So… if they locked you up and stuff… How did you get out? How did you… escape?"

Oh, she was not going to find it easy to accept the truth there, was she?

"They, uh, let me go," I said. Yep, confusion and

disbelief clouded her eyes once again. "David brought me back here," I added, figuring it was best to let it all out.

"But *why*? I mean, don't get me wrong, I'm just so *relieved*" — tears were flooding up in her eyes again — "that you're back, but it just, I mean, it doesn't make any sense!"

"Honestly…" I sighed. "I'm not so sure about that part myself. I thought it was weird as well, but I wasn't going to say *no*, you know?"

She nodded, her eyes once more returning to my injuries. Yeah, if I didn't have those, there was no way she would've believed any of that, despite it being more or less the truth.

She gulped. "Do you think they'll… come back?"

That was a good question. And one I didn't know how to answer. If I were them, I'd keep me under surveillance, just in case Luce showed up again, but I didn't know if they'd bother. Maybe they'd decided there was no more point? I certainly had no way of knowing unless I spotted Kit or David nearby.

"And where did they take you?" Lynn continued.

"I'm not sure. It was this place a few hours' drive away, I think." I rubbed the back of my neck uncomfortably. "And I really hope they won't show up again. I've kind of… had enough of cults for a lifetime."

"Maybe you should move," Lynn suggested, but I could hear from the doubt in her tone that she didn't believe I would. And she was right. I probably should, with both this cult and Paimon knowing where I lived. But both parties would always be able to find me again should they want to, and besides, I would never leave this house voluntarily. It was the only thing I had left of my uncle's. It was my home. It didn't have a large, fancy garden, or a pool, and it wasn't super close to work, but it was mine, and I loved it. So I shook my head.

"It wouldn't change anything."

Then I peered into Lynn's face, trying to determine just how much my kidnapping had affected her. "But how are you? I saw your texts when I got back…"

She bit her lip, tears welling up once more. This was going to be a very tearful evening, wasn't it? Seeing her like that made me choke up a little too. My wonderful best friend, who'd been so worried about me she would have moved Heaven and Earth if she could.

"I… well… I'm better now." She took my hand and squeezed it, even managing a small, quivering smile. "Taylor and I decided to postpone the wedding until we knew what had happened, but I guess that doesn't need to happen anymore. Well, if you're sure you're okay, that is."

Upon an impulse, I hugged her again.

"You don't need to postpone anything," I asserted. "I'm here for you and for all of this."

She nodded weakly but then looked up at me again, worry still clouding her eyes.

"What about Lucian?" Her lips were trembling again. "I haven't been able to reach him either. Do you think… That fight… Is he…?"

"He's fine," I said, desperately hoping it was true. "He saw David take me away, so I guess he thought I'd be safe and may be having a good time somewhere. He's got some stuff he needs to deal with, family matters, but he'll be okay and back before we know it. He sent me a text to let me know." I shrugged, chuckling uncomfortably. "But I only saw it today."

"Okay."

Then my stomach growled, and images of greasy and spicy food popped into my head. The food I'd gotten at the cult had been so incredibly bland, it could hardly even be called food. But a spicy pizza with pepperoni and chorizo on top along with some hot sauce… I could devour three large ones.

"Pizza?" I asked Lynn, and she nodded. I ordered quickly, and by the time it arrived, we'd gotten most of the crying out of the way and Lynn had shot a text to Taylor to let her know I was back. Lynn wanted to have me checked out at a hospital, but I refused. First of all, that would be insanely expensive, and secondly, it would include some uncomfortable questions, such as what massive creature had bitten me with fangs that large, and thirdly, I just didn't think it was necessary. If it hadn't gotten infected at this point, I was pretty sure I was safe.

I eventually convinced Lynn that filing a report and informing the cops was a waste of time. They'd write me off as a crazy lady. It wasn't like I had any evidence or witnesses to support my claims. Besides, I wouldn't have been surprised if Mother Leviticus had placed some of her underlings in the ranks of police and higher authorities. They'd need someone like that to cover up any encounter with a demon they found, after all.

We had our pizza while watching some funny videos on the internet, sorely needed to lift both our spirits, until Lynn needed to get home, and I needed to get some sleep so I could go back to work the next day.

Real normalcy was something I hadn't gotten to experience in quite a while, but over the course of the next five days, I went to work, had no offerings from demon stalkers, no break-ins, and no visits from the Devil. That actually counted as a record-breaking accomplishment.

Going back into work was a remarkably smooth process. People asked very few questions, mostly just if I was feeling better now, and I'd taken care to cover up the majority of my injuries with clothing.

Kit had left, of course, which no one was surprised about, but many of my colleagues regretted. I wondered how they'd feel if they ever met the real Kit. The beautiful badass Kit, instead of the beautiful but ditzy Kit.

I called my abuela to reassure her I was okay and continued to ignore any calls or texts from my dad. I also quickly got in touch with Brianna, since Lynn's bachelorette party had been scheduled for this coming weekend. Luckily, I'd filled Brianna in on the details before I'd been kidnapped, so when she'd found out I'd disappeared, she'd organized the last few missing pieces in my stead. I couldn't be more grateful to her. She didn't even ask many questions about my absence, accepting that Lynn knew what had happened, and that was all that mattered. I was starting to think she and I could become friends over all this.

I didn't hear at all from Luce. I thought about sending a text, but I didn't want to risk either the order intercepting my message somehow, or to distract Luce from whatever vital and dangerous thing might be happening in Hell right now. Finally, the weekend came around, and Brianna and I got ready at my house, discussing the last few details about our bachelorette party plan. Hailey had told Brianna that Taylor was having her party at the same time, so we'd decided to have a meet-up in the evening and finish the parties together.

"Sachets?" I read from our list.

"Check," Brianna said, holding up one of our mint-green ribbons.

"Extra set of clothing?"

"Check."

"Make-up kit?"

"Check."

"Painkillers?"

"Check."

"Tooty-horns?"

Brianna stopped and looked up at me, one eyebrow raised. "Tooty-horns?"

"Yeah, you know, those thingies that go…" I said and imitated an elephant. Badly.

"You mean a fanfare horn?"

I pointed my finger. "Yes, that!"

She sighed and held one up. "Check."

I read over my list again, then grinned at Brianna. "I think we're good to go."

We made it to Lynn's house in record time, and Taylor was already holding open the door for us so we could easily waltz in and grab our bride-to-be.

Our first stop was at an art atelier. Our model was already waiting for us, wearing nothing more than bathrobes. Buckets of paint and brushes were set out and ready, so we got right to it, painting a naked person. Well, it was more like painting *on* a naked person. She was our canvas and allowed us to cover her entire body in colors. She was very nice, laughing and joking with us, which took away the initial awkwardness almost instantly. The champagne also helped. As did the shots we took.

When we were done, we took a picture with her, and several of her and the paintings all across her body, including many, many rainbows.

And on we went to our cocktail-making class, where we not only learned how to make all sorts of cocktails, we also received a laminated recipe booklet for them at the end. Finally, giggling and drunk though we were, we reached our final stop for the day.

I ushered Brianna and Lynn into the club, Lynn still unaware of what kind of party awaited her. Just as I followed them in, I caught sight of a familiar face weaving through the crowd.

"Luce!" I shouted, forcing my way through the people to get to him. Something was off about him. He looked the same as always, his hair perfectly styled in that slightly intentionally messy way, his light-grey suit as dapper as ever, as if it had been freshly pressed, but his face told a different story. There was a troubled look in his eye, and his eyelids twitched a lot, as if he were afraid to blink, lest someone should attack him. He constantly surveyed the area, even after spotting me. His shoulders were pushed back and tenser than I'd ever seen them. He was wary, that much was clear.

"Luce," I repeated, "what's going on? Why are

you here?"

My hand found his arm, and he finally looked at me properly. His eyes flitted to my shoulder. Was it just me or was that relief in his face?

"I came to see you," he said quietly, yet I could still hear him perfectly clearly, despite the loud music that blasted through the space. My stomach jumped.

Wait, what?

"Were you able to… sort everything?" I asked, unsure whether to be relieved to see him, worried that there might be members of the order around, or terrified by what my stomach had just done.

Averting his gaze, he shook his head. "It's not over. Not by a long shot. He really wants you, you know?"

Something else entered his gaze when it returned to me, something I was too afraid to put a description to. Something that made my heart beat faster, my stomach jump some more, and weakened my knees.

Suddenly, Lynn was beside us, her shirt already covered in sprinkles of green paint from the party — yes, it was a paint party because what could be more perfect for her bachelorette party? — and threw her arms around Luce.

"Lucian! You made it! You two, I swear!" She looked from Luce to me and back again. "Between your collective disappearances, you'll make a girl grow old in a month!"

She grabbed us both by the hand and pulled us into the crowd toward Brianna. Luce looked at me, alarmed. "Disappearance?"

I shrugged and mouthed: *Later*.

And then, despite everything that had been going on and was still happening, we danced. Within minutes, we were just as covered in luminous paint as the thrashing people around us and took colorful shots out of vials with Brianna and Lynn. It didn't take long for Taylor and her own crew to appear, and we all ended up on the dance floor together, where Luce and I of course ended up creating another performance around which a circle of viewers formed.

Come on, how could anyone expect the two of us to just bop our heads to the music in a place like this? If we were going to dance, we were gonna do it right.

Except it felt different this time.

I couldn't tear my eyes from Luce, able to do nothing more than stare at him and wonder what was happening. I was worried. Very worried. The issue with Paimon wasn't resolved yet, and that meant that Luce wasn't safe. Paimon could show up here or take advantage of Luce's absence in Hell. I didn't even want to start thinking about the Order marching into the club to take on Luce.

And just as I'd finished thinking about how I *didn't* want to start thinking about it, I saw Kit and David. They weaved through the crowd, straight for us, while Luce and I were still mid-performance.

I spun closer to him.

"We have to go—now!" I hissed.

Something in my tone must have convinced him to act first and ask questions later because he grabbed me by the waist and held me tight. I closed my eyes as the world spun out of existence around us, and after a second, a heavy sulfuric smell engulfed us, which dissipated quickly. The sounds from the club were gone, leaving behind only our heavy breathing. I'd expected it to get cooler, but instead, I actually felt warmer than before. I felt sicker than I usually did after this method of travel, and I kept my eyes shut for another moment, just breathing in deeply to regain my composure.

"Ames?" Luce asked gently. "Are you okay?"

I nodded and clasped his shoulder. "Yup. Just give me a sec."

I hoped Lynn would forgive us for bailing on her party. Either because she was too drunk or happy to notice, or because I'd arranged for a spa day for tomorrow. Brianna would be with her at least.

Luce stroked my back, up and down, up and down, until, eventually, my nausea subsided, and I opened my eyes.

I didn't know what I'd expected to see. Perhaps my house, perhaps my office, but certainly not this.

We were standing in a vast desert, except it wasn't really a desert. It was a massive cave that looked like a desert. The floor was cracked from the heat, and there were rocks and boulders disturbing the world around us. Between them, flames shot up at irregular intervals. I stepped closer to Luce, and asked, even though I kind of knew the answer. "Where are we?"

"Hell," he replied, confirming my suspicions. "Part of the sixth circle. The nastier part."

Somehow, I'd hoped that the tales of Hell had been mostly made up and embellished by people over the years, but this place was unpleasant enough to fit the bill. So this was where I was doomed to exist for eternity once I died, huh?

Great.

I gulped but pulled myself together.

"Why here?" I asked. "Don't you have like… a castle or something?"

He nodded. "Pandæmonium. But, uh… It's not the best place to be right now. Paimon is… shall we say… performing a siege? Here is much safer. It's one of the most unpleasant regions in the rings, so we should be safe for a little while."

He pulled me beside one of the large rocks so we couldn't be snuck up on. But even then, he didn't let go of me. "What happened?"

I bit my lip. This was my chance to ask about Meredith, wasn't it? To find out how much of Kit and David's story was real. But first things first. "You know that friend you saw take me away?"
He nodded.

"That's David. He's part of a religious Order whose entire purpose is to find and kill you. So, to get you to come to them, he kidnapped me to try to lure you there. But that didn't work since you were, er, busy, so they let me go. But they must have still been following me because I saw some of their agents head straight for us at the club."

Luce nodded, not entirely surprised. "Ordo Sancti Matrem Suam?"

"Great, so you've met. Apparently, they're, uh, upset about a deal you made with a woman named Meredith?"

Luce's hand fell away from me, and he turned his eyes up at the cave ceiling far, far above us.

"Luce," I said quietly, "will you tell me what happened? Please, I want to know. It doesn't have to be now, but… later?"

He hesitated only for a moment, then nodded. "First, I think I… I think I need your help."

I blinked, playing his words over in my mind to check if I'd heard him right. "My help?"

The Devil needed my help? *My* help?

"Yeah. I need your strength. Whenever I'm with you, I feel more confident. Stronger. And I think that's just what I need right now to deal with," —he gestured to the world around us—"this."

Okay. So I was moral support. I could do that. Heck, if the Devil needed a cheerleader, I was definitely the girl for the job!

And that explained why he'd come back to the mundane world. He'd wanted to see me. To give him confidence. Somehow, knowing that made me a lot happier than I would have expected. A smirk had formed on my face, and it refused to go away, no matter how hard I tried.

Courage that I'd never known I had surged through my body, and I squeezed his hand. "Then let's go and show Paimon who's boss."

Chapter 16

I'd never expected to stare this many demons in the face at once. Certainly not within my lifetime. Luce had transported us to something that instantly translated to "throne room" in my mind, inside a crystal palace that I assumed was Pandæmonium. The throne, made from red, ruby-like crystal, was unoccupied, but Paimon in his demon shape stood beside it, one claw on its backrest, clearly itching to claim it. Why he wasn't already sitting on it, I didn't know, but I guessed it had something to do with the legitimacy of being ruler. For all I knew, it might turn an unworthy demon to ash. The throne was set up on a large dais, facing a wide hall, which was currently filled with demons. For some reason, Luce had elected to make us appear on the dais, on the other side of the ruby throne from Paimon. By all accounts, I was pretty sure that we had interrupted some grand speech. A part of me was almost sorry to have missed it, if only because I was extremely curious as to what type of pitchfork politics Paimon could use to create an uprising in a place like Hell.

Every single eye in the room was trained on us. I

could *feel* them turn their eyes to me as every hair on my body was raised.

Paimon's eyes had snapped to Luce when we appeared, but he'd remained still in his place. But when he noticed me, Paimon took a step toward us, the claw that had been resting on the chair now reaching toward me, hanging suspended in the air.

I gulped, inching closer to Luce. Playing moral support was all well and good, and the demon shapes really didn't bother me that much, but I *very* much didn't like the way Paimon was leering at me, especially after our last encounter. And I could definitely see some of the demons licking their mouths—calling them "lips" would have been generous.

Another point for the Queen of Bad Decisions: agreeing to come to the center of Hell to stop a demonic revolution in its tracks.

Luce took on his Devil shape as well, the piercing, flaming eyes, the horns, the split, pointed tail, the red skin and sharp teeth, along with an animalistic change in his body, making him more muscular and taller, as well as stretching the length of his arms.

"This is my throne," he growled, his voice taking on a certain multiplicity, as if a hundred voices were speaking simultaneously. "Paimon is not worthy of it."

"Human lover!" one of the demons in the crowd jeered. I had to assume it was meant to be an insult.

"You are straying from your purpose!" another added, followed by a cacophony of yells and shouts, most surrounding the idea that Luce preferred humans over demonkind, neglecting their needs.

"I promise that demonkind will have free rein to enter the human world whenever," Paimon finally said quietly because the room had instantly gone silent when he'd opened his mouth. "Demons will reign supreme over both worlds, and before long, we will take the Heavens as well. No one will stop us!"

A loud cheer erupted, and I tried to figure out why. There was no way that could work, was there? Not if God and his army of angels were real. And besides, hadn't Paimon started all this specifically so he could own me? Was he only promising them these things because he knew that was what they wanted? But how soon would he turn on that? How soon would he decide it wasn't worth it? How much of the truth had he told them? Something I had never questioned before was how capable angels were of lying. Luce could tell fibs, that much I had seen, so the same probably counted for Paimon.

And suddenly I realized something only I could do.

I squeezed Luce's hand before letting go and stepped forward.

"Excuse me, um, hello?" I said. The demons stared at me, their bodies tense, some frowning, others baring fangs at me. Paimon's eyes were trained on me and filled with greed.

"Ames," Luce warned quietly. "What are you doing?"

I turned to him for a moment and smiled, a lot more confidently than I was feeling. "Helping. I think."

This was such a bad idea. But I had to try.

"Um, hi, all." I addressed the crowd again. "Human here, as you may have gathered."

They were silent, waiting to see what I was going to say, but I had no doubts that if they didn't like what they heard, they'd tear me to shreds in seconds. But then I'd still be here, wouldn't I? Because my soul was going to come here anyway.

"Before I continue, I'd like to remind you that we're in the presence of an angel — several, actually — which means that I, as a human, literally cannot lie."

I waited for some acknowledgement from the demons and received a nod or two.

"Who cares?" one demon shouted. "You're nothing more than a snack!"

Before I could even determine which demon had spoken, the crowd was getting rowdy again, and more shouts followed in the same vein of the first.

"If it weren't for you there wouldn't be a problem!"

Oh, no.

Faster than I could react, several demons had decided that that the easiest resolution would be to remove the one and only obstacle: me. Some demons with spikes along their spines or more limbs than a spider would have pushed through the crowd, but one of them batted above the crowd on massive beetle-like wings and charged me from the air, fangs gnashing.

I saw my own death play out in front of me, my biggest regret that I wouldn't be there for Lynn's wedding day. But at the last second, Luce stepped in front of me and, one arm raised, froze the demon midair. The room fell silent again instantly.

"You will listen to what she has to say," he commanded.

Wow. Unhappy with him or not, he was still their ruler, and the power he held over them was undeniable. Gathering all my courage, trusting that Luce would keep me safe no matter what, I stepped out from behind him once more. Time to finish what I started.

"Okay, so, how many of you are here because you don't like that Luce—I mean Lucifer—is in the human realm so much?"

I got no reaction aside from a few growls and fierce glares. Behind me, Luce cleared his throat. A few talons, claws, and hands rose, and I nodded, satisfied that Luce's words had coerced them into compliance for the moment.

"How many of you have been explicitly forbidden from going?"

None raised their claws.

"How many of you just don't see a point in going up because of specific rules concerning your interactions with, er, mortals or otherwise?"

A lot of demons demonstrated their agreement.

"Okay. How many of you are angry because of what Paimon told you about Lucifer's behavior?"

Most demons agreed. There was even some murmuring. As it turned out, this was going very similarly to what I'd expected.

I took a deep breath.

"In that case, let me tell you something about both of them." I pointed at Luce and Paimon. "And remember, I can't lie. Yes, Lucifer spends a lot of time around humans. But he also thinks about the best way forward for you, and Hell in general. Have any of you truly had problems because Luce was your ruler?"

No one reacted.

"I didn't think so. Now, I guess I can sort of understand why you're not happy that Lucifer has attachments to humans. In fact, when Paimon and I met, he pretty much told me as much. He couldn't understand it, so he didn't like it. But guess what: Paimon is in the same boat."

"Stop." Paimon growled, and he was on me, pushing me to the floor, standing over me, his fiery gaze fierce and angry.

"He's started this revolution because he wants to

have a human to himself," I continued, looking right back at him, knowing that if I stopped now, my fate was not only sealed, but everything I'd done would be in vain. If Paimon truly wanted me, he couldn't kill me, not yet. Not until he was Ruler of Hell. I shot Luce a glance, to stop him from jumping in like he'd done before. Not this time.

"Me," I concluded, and Paimon growled, his fangs glinting menacingly in the light of the fires refracted by the crystals around us. A drop of his spit splashed right next to my face.

"Additionally," I called out, "did you see how hastily he reacted just now? Do you really want to have a leader who acts so impulsively, or someone who thinks things through? Think about what's at stake here. Total domination over the realms sounds all nice and well, but then what? And do you really think the Heavens will be as easily beaten as Paimon seems to think?

"He's telling you what you want to hear, but his words are empty. He's irrational and power-hungry. He's greedy. In short, he's like a child who hasn't learned to care about anything but himself. And is that really who you want as your ruler?"

The longer I spoke, the angrier Paimon got. He'd already pinned down both my arms with his, and the flames in his eyes were sparking and cracking an icy blue. He was about to snap. And when he did, I was in a very bad place.

"The lady's right, you know," a very soothing, smooth voice said. "Paimon's always been so loyal to our lord. Why do you think he would suddenly turn, if not for something he wants above everything else? Look at him now. He hasn't even found the strength to devour her yet."

Paimon gave a primal screech, and opened his mouth, baring his fangs to dart at me, but before he could reach my neck, he was flicked away. A very graceful androgynous figure stepped into his place. It looked like a creature somewhere between a fox, a deer, and a person, and they extended a hand to help me up, their fluffy, reddish tail swishing, pleased, from side to side.

"Just think about how pitifully weak he is. The only reason why he hasn't lost yet is because our dearest Lord Lucifer cares for him, the same way he cares for all of you."

A moment later, Luce was beside me, looking me over for new injuries. A little unnerved, I smiled at him to reassure him I was okay. Though I wasn't going to lie, getting knocked down had made my already existing injuries flare up a little, especially since they'd already been tested during Lynn's bachelorette party.

Once Luce was satisfied of my condition, he walked over to the throne and took his seat upon it. A blinding light began to radiate from it, engulfing the entire room before subsiding again. The demons fell to their knees—or equivalents thereof—to show their allegiance, including the fox-deer person.

Paimon was huddled in a corner, defeat written across every part of him.

I wasn't sure how exactly this had resolved the situation, but it seemed to have happened. And that was a good thing, right?

I looked at Luce, as the only person not prostrating myself before him, and he beckoned me closer. When I was within reach of him, he simply picked me up and pulled me onto his lap, holding me tightly.

Woops, there my stomach was again, this time seemingly playing an internal version of hula-hoops.

"Paimon," Luce said. "You made a choice. I respect that. But you will also have to bear the consequences of that choice."

Paimon scuttled in front of us, nodding, ashamed. Seriously, it was *that* easy?

"You will continue to be one of the Kings of Hell. But this human"—Luce stroked my hair—"is mine. Her soul belongs to me, and me alone, and I will keep her by my side forever. Do you understand?"

So, obviously I'd sold my soul to Luce, so I quite literally belonged to him, but I kind of got the impression that he wasn't talking about that. I watched Luce's face, wondering if it was anti-feminist of me if I thought that I really didn't mind him saying that I belonged to him.

But did he belong to me?

Wow, where had that thought come from?

I was starting to get flustered just listening to my internal monologue and my face was growing warmer with every moment. He was the *Devil!* Seriously, I was going to have to see a doctor after all, regardless of how much it cost me. Something must have been wrong with me.

Luce looked over his subjects and then addressed the fox-deer person.

"Asmodeus, please deal with this, would you?" He gestured at the hall. "There is something else I need to take care of."

Asmodeus bowed and winked at me, just before Luce and I once more transported, this time to my house. My living room, in fact, where David and Kit were already waiting for us, weapons raised and all. How they'd known we'd come back there tonight was beyond me, but I could imagine it had been mostly guess work and perhaps at least some observation of Luce's past behavior. It was my home, after all.

David had a gun trained at Luce's head, and I swore there was a fancy cross etched into its side. Meanwhile, Kit held a dagger, with three more waiting for their moment in a sheath at her side.

I gulped, still feeling nauseous, though in this moment, I wasn't sure if it was because of this situation or because of the jump. The first morning light was already tweaking through the blinds, but I barely had a thought to spare for it.

"Um, hi," I said, though my knees were trembling a little.

Crap. Luce was even still in his Devil form, wasn't he? The shape that David and Kit knew as the downfall of their ancestor. It had been immortalized in their crypt, after all.

Luce was still holding me, and I was clutching on to him tightly in return. What was I meant to do in a situation like this? Say I could explain? It wasn't what it looked like? Except that it was. The Devil was standing right in front of them.

"This isn't what it looks like," Luce said.

Ugh.

"Then what are we looking at?" Kit asked, and it was impossible for anyone to stare harder daggers than she was doing right now.

"From what I've gathered over the years" — Luce shook his head, sadly — "you have quite the misconception about your relationship to me. Or my relationship to you. Your curse is a self-fulfilling prophecy, but I'm not the one causing the demise of your family."

I stared at him, confused about what he meant. If nothing else, it proved that he was definitely aware of their family, recognized them, even. He knew what was going on with them.

Kit narrowed her eyes, but she didn't respond.

Instead, she attacked.

She lunged at Luce, two daggers drawn and ready to plunge into his flesh, but with a single movement of his arm, he blocked the attack without even touching her and sent her across the room against the wall. The TV fell off its mount and crashed to the floor, the screen cracking into a million tiny pieces.

"Oops." He winced, glancing at me guiltily. "I didn't mean to use that much force."

Right now, I honestly had more important things to worry about than a TV. Like David, who was still pointing his gun at Luce's head.

David's hands were shaking, and he barely managed to keep the gun straight. A bead of sweat rolled across his temple as he stared at Luce. I couldn't blame him for being afraid. Luce did look terrifying and after what had just happened with Kit's attack… I pried myself loose from Luce and rushed over to her side. She'd crashed onto the floor and had received a nasty wound to the head from the impact. I really didn't want to imagine how much force Luce had used, because I was pretty sure that it was more then Paimon had used when he'd swiped me away two weeks ago, and that had hurt like hell.

Kit was breathing steadily, but she was unconscious, which I believed was a blessing, considering the circumstances, but I still moved her into a more stable position, before reverting my attention to the two men stuck in a stalemate.

"David," I called out. "Don't. Let him explain, please?"

David's lips trembled and twitched, but he didn't move, his eyes still glued to Luce.

"Luce? Maybe shift to a less-threatening shape?" I suggested helpfully.

"Oh? You think it'll help?" He looked at me, almost surprised.

I shrugged. "It might."

A moment later, he was back to his dapper-looking human self and moved to sit in the armchair, directing David to the couch. Hesitantly, and evidently a little confused, David lowered his gun, but he didn't move to sit down.

Fine, then. I walked over and grabbed one of the pillows to place under Kit's neck before working to bandage that wound on her head. It wasn't bleeding too much, so she wasn't in any life-threating danger. She was still going to need an ambulance, but I had a feeling that David would prefer to take her back to the Order instead.

"This is all about my interactions with Merry, isn't it?" Luce asked

"Meredith," David corrected. "My ancestor."

Luce nodded, looking up to the ceiling, seemingly reminiscing.

"We're good friends, Merry and I."

"She made a deal with you," David said, his eyes narrowing menacingly.

Luce leaned forward in his seat, propping up his elbows on his knees and putting his hands together. "Yes, she did. But do you know the contents of that deal?"

"All I know is that she forfeited the souls of all her descendants for whatever deal you tricked her into."

Luce shook his head sadly. "I never trick anyone. I take excessive precautions to make sure that everyone who receives one of my deals knows exactly what they're signing away. Ames can attest to that."

He gestured to me, and when David glanced my way, I nodded.

"And no one can sign away someone else's soul. Everyone has to make their own choices, their own decisions, and deal with their own repercussions."

"Then how do you explain everyone in my family dying by forty?"

"As I mentioned, it's a self-fulfilling prophecy. Your family seeks out demons to fight. Naturally, those demons will defend themselves, and as you've just witnessed"—Luce pointed to Kit—"we sometimes find it difficult to gauge our strength with respect to humans. Which means that most of your family dies young because you're constantly going after beings stronger than you."

Luce sighed, and it was such a deep sigh, I could feel all the sadness and regret behind it.

"And as for the rest… Meredith's deal… It was a

gift to her descendants. She gave up her own soul, so each one of her descendants could have the chance to wish for something without having to pay a price. She gave up her soul so all of you could receive an angel's blessing. Unfortunately, it seems that whenever I offered that blessing, your family members thought they'd failed their holy mission, and they… sent me away, before killing themselves so they wouldn't need to live with the shame. Though I believe there are some that simply staged their own death and ran away. There's only been one person to accept the blessing so far."

I was staring at Luce just as hard as David was. *What…?*

How strongly did this family believe in Luce being evil that they would kill themselves if he offered them a gift…? Then again, looking at Kit and remembering how fiercely she'd spoken about the deal in the crypt… It wasn't entirely implausible.

"But…" David wasn't resisting the truth entirely. He must have felt the truth behind Luce's words, possibly remembering things his family had said, thinking about how he himself would react if Luce had shown himself. "But the angel…"

His voice was weak, and he was desperately clinging on to the last mysteries not yet solved. The angel. Who was also Luce.

We shared a look and I nodded. Then, Luce transformed again, this time to his original form, the one God had given him, created him with. The one of a terrifying angel.

His eyes were like torches, and six giant wings framed his figure that wasn't altogether humanoid anymore but wasn't so far away from it as not to be recognizable, either. I couldn't look at his face. Everything disappeared when I did, except for the terrifying flames that seemed to burn the fabric of the universe itself. There were rings moving around him that were a part of him, covered in eyes that watched the world, watched all of it with horrifying intensity.

I closed my eyes, forcing myself to regulate my breathing. Out of his three shapes, this one was the only one that had ever scared me. And it still did. It was ancient, full of power and knowledge. If Lovecraft's creatures had been based on reality, he'd have written about Lucifer's angelic form.

"Shit," David whispered as he sank to the floor.

"Do you see now?" Lucifer, the Morning Star, son of God, asked gently, his voice sounding as if every human on Earth had spoken in unison.

"I… I do." David sighed, defeated, and yet… perhaps relieved?

"Then I look forward to what you'll ask of me in four years."

Luce's voice was back to normal.

I opened my eyes to see him standing there in his human shape, watching David. Luce's gaze was soft, a small smile on his lips. My heart grew warm at seeing his compassion, and I crossed the room, until my head was leaning against Luce's collarbone and my hands wrapped around his torso. One of his arms moved around my back as well, holding me gently.

David took a few minutes to collect himself, but then he lifted himself off the floor and walked over to Kit, picking her up before heading toward the door.

There, he turned around again. "My hunt is over. I choose to believe you. But I can't guarantee that it'll be the same for her, or anyone else."

Luce nodded. "I know."

"If you show them this form… It might change things," David put forward before he left, but Luce shook his head, gaze cast to the ground.

"It doesn't. I've tried."

David watched him for a moment without expression. Then he nodded.

Having witnessed for himself just how terrifying Luce's original shape was, he must have realized that even the carving in their crypt couldn't prepare anyone for the sight. He glanced to me. "Goodbye, Amelia."

And that was it. David left. Luce and I sank onto the couch, both exhausted from the last few hours.

"So what happened to Meredith?" I asked, tilting my head to one side. "She's in Hell now, right?"

"She sure is. She has a lake house with Asmodeus in the eighth circle."

"A lake house?" I couldn't believe my ears, trying

to combine the imagery of a lake house with the desolate wasteland I had seen. No way. Not unless it was a lake made of fire and magma.

Luce chuckled. "Believe it or not, you actually saw the worst part of Hell. There's plenty nicer parts. Your human stories about Hell and Heaven are mostly wrong. Mostly. There are some exceptions, I suppose."

"Right."

Suddenly, I was curious about seeing the rest of Hell. I wondered if I should ask him to take me for a tour some time, or if it was better to wait until I was confined there for eternity. But now was not the time. Now, I was just tired.

"You're a lot of trouble, you know that?" I sighed. "When you're around, I never have a quiet moment."

He chuckled. "But you haven't told me to beat it yet."

I smiled. "I guess not. By the way, Lynn told me I'm not allowed to show up without a date to the wedding and that's in a few weeks, so you're gonna have to make up for it by going with me."

Winking, he gave me a thumbs up. "You got it."

Epilogue

"I do," Taylor said.

"I do, too," Lynn responded, her voice trembling with overwhelming happiness.

I watched from the sidelines as they exchanged their rings, both brides radiating joy. It was easy to smile along. How could I not be happy to see my best friend marry the love of her life?

The day was perfect. All the dresses were on point, the décor of the old castle chapel was beautiful, and the flowers I'd picked out for the corsages and bouquets worked in perfect harmony. So far there hadn't been any hiccups in or around the ceremony.

The bridal pair kissed, and the chapel erupted in cheers. I probably cheered the loudest. Lynn deserved all the happiness in the world.

Lynn and Taylor left the chapel, all bridesmaids and Luce following before the rest of the guests left as well. I hurried over to the usher to tell him to guide the guests toward the reception hall before hurrying back so I was ready for the bridal party photographs once Lynn and Taylor were done with greetings and well-wishers.

Seeing that they were currently busy with Taylor's grandparents, I strolled over to Luce, who, waiting at the side of the chapel, looked very dapper in his silver suit. I hadn't had a chance to speak with him since that night. He'd left shortly after David had because he'd needed to make sure Hell really was back to normal. He'd been there since then, leaving me to deal with Lynn's wrath about leaving the bachelorette party early on my own. Luckily, she'd quickly forgiven us, especially when she'd found out that I'd paid for a whole spa day for her and Brianna and promised her that we could have one of our own after her honeymoon.

"Hey," I said.

"Hey." He grinned back at me.

"How's Hell?"

"Oh, you know. Full of fiery pits. Tortured souls. Demons. The usual."

I rolled my eyes. "Ha-ha."

His smirk grew wider. "It's fine. And you won't need to worry about Paimon anymore. I've given him a job that should help him relieve him of his frustration."

I decided not to ask. I really didn't want to know. So instead, I changed the subject.

"How come you're standing here all alone? I would have bet money on the fact that you'd be surrounded by women pretty much every free moment. What happened? Lost your charm?"

"I decided I only wanted to charm one woman," he said seriously, looking deep into my eyes.

My teasing grin froze on my lips as my stomach started making summersaults and conducting an entire circus routine.

"Um," I said, very intelligently.

Then Luce winked at me. "Save me a dance," he whispered as he walked past me.

Oh, damn. I'd convinced myself that it had just been the excitement, the jumping from place to place, heck, even the alcohol, but after the time that had passed since then, all of that should have gone away. Which meant there was only one possible reason why my body was reacting this way to Luce.

I liked him. And not just as a friend.

I'd held my speech and now it was time for cake. Lynn's mint cake had actually made it onto the top tier of their three-tier cake. Smiling, I shook my head as I partook in carrot cake instead. Meanwhile, Lynn, who was next to me, shoveled mint cake into her mouth like she'd never had anything better in her life.

"Just couldn't resist, huh?" I asked.

She shrugged. "Can you blame me? It's so good! And seeing as we had the option for multiple cakes…"

I snorted. "Taylor couldn't say *no* to that face you make, could she?"

"Whatever do you mean? This one?" She gave me her best pleading eyes, complete with eyelid batting and pouty lips. Her makeup only made it more effective.

"That's the one."

"Well, it's so effective, how could I not?" She grinned, cheekily, and we both giggled. Then, she grew serious again and raised an eyebrow. "You didn't bring a date."

"I brought Luce," I protested. "Like I said I would."

"But he was going to be here anyway." She groaned. "And he's not a date, he's like your backup."

I glanced over at him talking to Brianna, but when he noticed me staring, he smiled at me and raised his glass. I hadn't looked away from a man this quickly since I'd been in high school.

"Yup," I said, trying to convince myself that it was true. But I was pretty sure that my warming face betrayed me. "My backup."

Lynn gasped and threw her hand over her mouth. "Oh, my god, you *like* him, don't you? After everything, you finally like him?"

"Shh!" I glanced around, hoping that no one had heard her outburst, especially not the Devil in question.

"Look at you, you're even blushing! I haven't seen you blush since…" She paused, trying to figure out how to say "since Jonathan" without actually saying it. "Years ago," she finally settled. Then she gasped again. "Is that why you ditched my party? Did you two…?"

"What? Oh my god, no! No, we didn't! Hell, Lynn, you really think I'd do that to you?"

She shrugged. "You disappeared and still haven't told me why."

"But I did promise you another spa day if you let it go," I reminded her. "And I'm still super, mega sorry. But I promise you, we really didn't have much of a choice."

"So you said." She narrowed her eyes at me, but I knew it was mostly playful.

I rolled my eyes and got up, tapping Brianna on the shoulder as I did.

"Where are you going?" Lynn protested and I threw a smirk back at her.

"We prepared a little surprise."

Brianna, Hailey, and Chrissy one of Taylor's other bridesmaids, and I got into position on the dance floor in front of the bridal pair. Luce started the music, and we plunged into our choreographed dance.

I'd come up with it myself, some ideas that I'd developed while my brain had had nothing better to do during a week of being locked up, and when I'd gotten home, I'd taken a video and sent it to the other bridesmaids. Luckily, they'd liked the idea and had learned the dance in the meantime, so performing it now was no big deal. We'd only rehearsed it once all together yesterday, but it had gone pretty well.

By the end of our twirls and twists, deafening applause rang in our ears and there were tears in the brides' eyes. I wiggled my eyebrows at Lynn, and she shook her head, laughing.

Luce walked up to me and handed me the microphone.

"That was fantastic," he said, leaning in, and I smiled before bringing the microphone to my lips. "Thank you, esteemed guests! This was a little performance we bridesmaids made up for our wonderful friends Lynn and Taylor." I paused to let the applause die away. "And now I would like to ask the newlyweds to the dance floor so I can present to you all, for the first time ever, Mrs. and Mrs. Haleston!"

I joined in the applause, leaving the dance floor to make space for the brides.

Their first dance was a slow waltz, and even though they both just swayed from side to side, it was magical.

The moment the next song began, Luce stood in front of me, holding out his hand to me and smiling. "May I ask for this dance?"

My heart leapt to my throat, even though I'd known this would happen. I placed my hand in his and let him guide me to the dance floor.

With every step we took, I was aware of how close he was to me, of where his body touched mine, and I was beginning to find it difficult to breathe. I felt like I really was back in high school.

"I like you," I blurted out.

Luce's grin widened. "Well, I'm glad to hear that," he said, pulling me closer to him. "Because I meant what I said to Paimon in Hell, you know."

His words echoed back in my head.

I will keep her by my side forever.

He leaned into me, and I into him, our lips meeting in a long-overdue kiss.

His lips were firm, and they matched mine perfectly, guiding me into the sweetest yet most passionate kiss I'd ever experienced.

Yeah, I'd sold my soul to the Devil.

But it had taken me until now to realize I'd also given him my heart.

Thank you!

I hope you had as much fun reading *Devil Deal* as I had writing it.

It should go without saying that you shouldn't take any of its contents too seriously. While some aspects may be based of certain religions that shall remain nameless here, they are by no means true to the corresponding texts, nor did I intend them to be.

As always, I'd like to sincerely thank everyone who had a hand in the creation of this book.

Now that that's out of the way—this book is actually a gift to my Lynn, though she's really called Trina, and her partner Sam.

Congratulations to you both!

More By Janina Franck

<u>**Short Stories**</u>

The Weight of Time (*A Touch of Magic, 2019*)
A Spark in Space (*A Touch of Magic, 2019*)
Override (*Brave New Girls: Girls who Tech and Tinker, 2020*)
Káto Kósmos (*Sing, Goddess!, 2021*)
The Wizard's Bride (*Space Bound, 2021*)
Midnight Train (*Beyond, 2022*)

<u>**Novels**</u>

The Chronicles of the Bat
Captain Black Shadow (*2016*)
White Devil (*2019*)
Sand and Snow (*2020*)

A Spark in Space: A Space Witch Novel (*2021*)

Crimson Fox Publishing is an independent, author-driven publisher of New Adult and Adult fiction of all genres. We were founded in 2020 by authors from Snowy Wings Publishing and its former sister imprints, Animus Ferrum Publishing and Caleo Press, using the unique co-op model developed by SWP.

Our Mission

We are an UN-traditional publisher focused on providing authors with a team that supports and boosts each other, while also enabling each author flexibility and independence. In a time when the publishing industry is in a constant state of flux, we strive to chart our own course and find a new way that unites traditional and independent publishing to bring our works to all readers, whether they be committed Kindle owners, print book hoarders, or library lovers.

www.ingramcontent.com/pod-product-compliance
Lightning Source LLC
Chambersburg PA
CBHW060914190726

48286CB00002B/493